He took a step toward her.

A hot tide of longing ran through Tracy. She might not trust her feelings, but she couldn't deny them. She still wanted Judd with all the wild yearning of long ago.

She fought it and knew he was doing the same.

He faced her, all iron control now. The tough sheriff in a tough situation. "You might be in charge of the case, but I'm still sheriff of this county. If your life is in danger, I'm going to do my damnedest to see that you aren't hurt...no matter what."

He went out, cutting through the woods in the moonlight. The pressure was building between them. When it got too great, what would happen?

She wanted to leave. She wanted to solve the case and get out of there...before it was too late.

Laurie Paige

was recently presented with the *Affaire de Coeur*
Readers' Choice Silver Pen Award for Favorite
Contemporary. In addition, she is a Romance
Writers of America 1994 RITA finalist for Best
Traditional Romance for her book, *Sally's Beau*.
She's also had another super event—the birth
of her first grandchild, a boy. "Definite hero
material!"

To Jill Barnett—for Keegan
To Jane Bonander—for Kerrigan
And to Georgina Devon—for reading
through all of it

Laurie Paige

THE ONCE AND FUTURE WIFE

Silhouette Books

Published by Silhouette Books

America's Publisher of Contemporary Romance

Special thanks and acknowledgment to
Laurie Paige for her contribution to the
Montana Mavericks series.

Text and artwork on page 8 is reprinted with permission from
NEVER ASK A MAN THE SIZE OF HIS SPREAD:
A Cowgirl's Guide to Life, by Gladiola Montana.
Copyright © 1993 Gibbs Smith Publisher. All rights reserved.

SILHOUETTE BOOKS

ISBN 0-373-50168-4

THE ONCE AND FUTURE WIFE

Copyright © 1994 by Harlequin Enterprises B.V.

Printed in U.S.A.

MONTANA
Mavericks

*Welcome to Whitehorn, Montana—
the home of bold men and daring women.
A place where rich tales of passion and
adventure are unfolding under the Big Sky.
Seems that this charming little town has some mighty
big secrets. And everybody's talking about...*

Homer Gilmore: A harmless hermit, he's been wandering around Whitehorn for longer than anyone can remember. And he may be the silent witness to some strange goings-on. Can anyone believe his stories? Especially a lawman like...

Officer Rafe "Wolf Boy" Rawlings: Dark and brooding, his life has been one big question mark. Now the discovery of the mysterious bones found on the Laughing Horse Reservation could signal the end to his elusive past. But nobody can help him unravel the clues, not even...

Winona Cobbs: Wily old Winona, town seer, doesn't have all the answers. But her mind is filled with images, and her soul is haunted by visions—of a woman with two faces...

Mary Jo Kincaid: She married a rich man and is sitting pretty. A relative newcomer, she has special interest in Whitehorn's colorful history—especially the old rumors about the disappearance of...

Lexine Baxter: Turns out she's more that just a name on a missing person's report. This hell-raiser has a wild history— and an obsession with a lost sapphire mine....

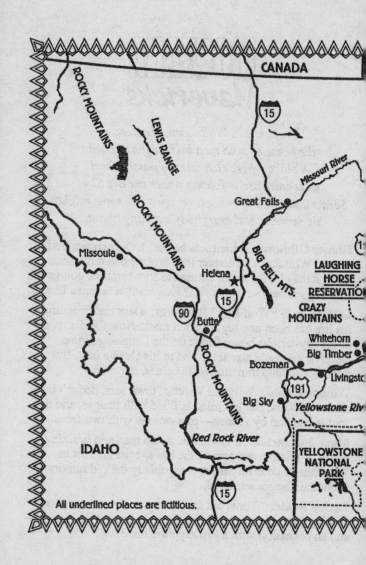

CANADA

15

ROCKY MOUNTAINS

LEWIS RANGE

Missouri River

Great Falls

Missoula

ROCKY MOUNTAINS

BIG BELT MTS.

Helena

15

90

Butte

LAUGHING
HORSE
RESERVATION

CRAZY
MOUNTAINS

Whitehorn

Big Timber

Bozeman

ROCKY MOUNTAINS

191

Livingsto

Big Sky

Yellowstone Riv

Red Rock River

IDAHO

YELLOWSTONE
NATIONAL
PARK

15

All underlined places are fictitious.

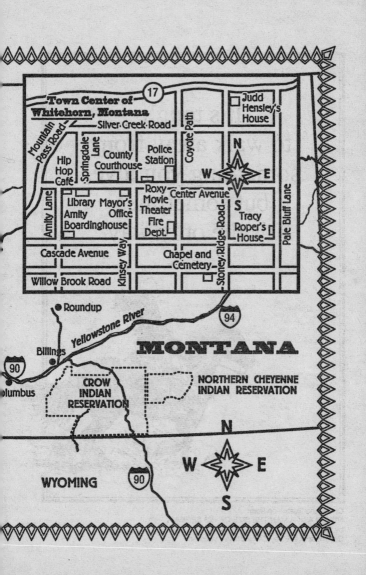

It's tough
to walk away from
something you love,
but sometimes
it's the only way.

One

Tracy Roper parked across the street from the police station. She sat in the car, her hands locked on the steering wheel as she let her gaze drift along the busy avenue, past the mayor's house on the corner; past the Roxy Theater, where she'd gone to summer movies with friends; past the real-estate office where she was to pick up the key to the rental house.

From where she was on Center Avenue, it was only a couple of blocks, then a left turn onto another street and a short drive to the last house on the right before the county-road intersection....

A tremor ran through her as she realized where her thoughts were taking her. Once upon a time she'd lived in that house on Stoney Ridge Road...so long ago it sometimes seemed like a dream.

Or a nightmare.

Squeals of laughter reached her through the closed windows of her compact car. She glanced down the block toward the town park, where three children played on the swings. Their mothers sat on the wooden benches that lined the play area, chatting and laughing while they kept an eye on their young charges.

For a minute, Tracy's eyes lingered on a toddler, a busy little boy whose dark hair gleamed with auburn highlights in the morning sun. When he fell in the sand, her heart lurched and her hands tightened in a painful grip.

The child's mother scooped him up in a soothing embrace and dried his tears. Tracy glanced away.

Pulling down the sun visor, she checked her face in the mirror. She looked okay, she decided. Her makeup seemed fresh enough from when she'd put it on at six that morning at her father's house in Missoula.

She'd visited him over the weekend before driving down to Whitehorn to begin her latest task—checking out some bones found on the Laughing Horse Reservation.

The tribal police and the county sheriff's office were in contention over who was in charge of the case, so the federal government had been called in. As a forensic anthropologist for the FBI, she would have full control of the investigation.

Sighing, she admitted she was putting off the moment she would have to face Judd Hensley, the county sheriff— the man who'd been her husband . . . the father of her child. . . .

She picked up her purse, opened the car door and climbed out into the hot late-June sunshine. The breeze was crisp, blowing off mountains where clouds were gathering for an afternoon rain.

Before she could cross the street, a couple came out of the station and stood on the steps. She stopped as if struck by lightning.

Judd.

The sun glanced off his shining black hair with its smooth wave brushed back from his forehead. His skin was evenly, darkly tanned. The first time she'd seen him she'd thought he was an Indian.

So long ago . . . that magical summer when she'd been nineteen and thought all the world was in love. Seventeen years . . .

He'd been kneeling by the creek when she'd rounded a bend in the trail and spotted him. She'd stopped, surprised, alarmed and fascinated as he scooped up water and drank it from his hand. It had dribbled over his chest and belly.

He'd been buck naked.

She'd thought he was a savage or a character from an ancient fable somehow transported through aeons to this moment. She'd known in an instant that she'd never forget him.

He'd whipped his head around, sensing her presence. His eyes, as dark and alluring as forbidden knowledge, had taken in all aspects of her, including her soul, in one glance. He'd stood and turned in one smooth, sinuous movement.

His body had been fully erect, a symbol of the power and creative force contained within him.

Pagan, she'd thought, spellbound by his special magic.

She'd stood very still, as if in the presence of a mythical creature, not wanting to startle him into disappearing. They'd stared into each other's eyes for an eternity.

Then he'd spoken, his voice a deep rumble of concern and assurance. "Don't be afraid," he'd murmured.

He'd said the same thing two weeks later when they'd made love for the first time...

Laughter broke into her memories.

Judd's teeth gleamed strong and white against his tan while he laughed at something his companion said. The woman—Maris Wyler, Tracy decided, delving into her memories for a name to go with the face—reached up and caressed his cheek before running lightly down the steps and climbing into a truck at the curb.

Tracy watched his gaze follow the truck. The smile that had lingered on his passionately mobile mouth disappeared. A tight-lipped expression took its place. He swung his head in her direction suddenly.

Judd had thought he was prepared to meet Tracy again. It had been years since he'd seen her. The pain had long since subsided into the empty place inside him where nothing could hurt.

But he hadn't counted on this. The impact of seeing her was like getting hit with a slug from a buffalo gun. He tightened one hand into a fist, angered by the reaction that raged through his body. He watched as she left her car and approached the crosswalk.

She wore a golden yellow suit with a blouse printed in random splotches of red, blue and yellow. Her belt, heels and purse were the same shade as the blue in the blouse. Her earrings were blue flowers with golden centers. She looked like Spring personified.

Her hair was light auburn. It gleamed like copper wire in the sun, but he knew its real texture. It was the same shade, the same downy softness, wherever he'd touched it on her body.

A harsh pang of need drove through him like a heat-tempered spear. He knew exactly what she looked like without the city clothes and the makeup that highlighted her green eyes.

The mountain wind made wanton love to her as she paused, her gaze going in one direction, then the other, as she waited for a break in the bustling Monday-morning traffic.

Her skirt, coaxed by the wind, pressed between her thighs, outlining the long slender grace of her legs . . . legs that had once wrapped sensuously around him, demanding he give himself to her completely, holding nothing back. And he had. God, he had!

She'd taken possession of his heart and soul. She'd wound herself around him until no moment was complete without her. Then she'd rejected him, scorning him as if their marriage had become an abomination, his touch so distasteful she couldn't bear it.

He'd waited, making no demands, ignoring his own pain, knowing they both needed to heal after the death of their son, but their time had never come again. It had been the final grief.

By the time of the divorce, it had been a relief to move out. By then, he'd felt like a dry husk of a man, empty, drained, with nothing left inside to give, even if she had wanted him again.

She never had. She'd left, not returning once during the seven years since the divorce. He forced the unwanted feelings into abeyance. It was better to be empty. Life was easier.

Tracy crossed the street, her two-inch heels clicking noisily on the pavement. She should have worn flats, but she would have felt short next to Judd's six-feet-plus frame, even though she was a bit over five-seven herself. She needed to feel in control, not like that foolish teenager who'd thought physical attraction was enough to build a life on.

The station steps had an iron railing running down the middle of them. She started up the right side of it. Judd was on the other side. He started down. They met in the middle.

He moved down one more step, so that they stood eye-to-eye. His hand brushed hers on the railing as he paused. A flash of sensation raced across her skin, almost like a pain.

"Hello, Tracy," he said, moving his hand farther up the railing. The other settled below where she gripped the smooth iron like a lifeline. "How are you?"

She stared at their hands, his tanned skin dark next to her paleness. There were tiny black hairs on the backs of his hands. His fingers were well-shaped, long and slender...sensuous.

A strange shiver ran over her, as if she could feel them caressing her, running down her breasts, her ribs, her stomach, her thighs....

With a gasp, she tore her gaze from those hands whose touch she'd once loved more than anything. "Fine," she finally answered. "And you?"

He shrugged. His shoulders were broad. He wore the uniform of the county sheriff well, at ease with the authority it imparted.

The dark brown shirt with the gold-silver-and-black badge that stated his official status hugged his muscular torso with great accuracy. The dark brown stripe up the side of the light brown pants made his legs seem even longer and more powerful.

A sudden memory came to her, sensual and compelling. During the cold Montana winters, he'd always slept close to her, his leg thrown across her thighs, his arm over her waist. Once he'd murmured it was too bad they didn't live at the North Pole so he could hold her close every night of the year.

She felt the warming of her body, the softness creeping inside her, the moist heat forming as she prepared to receive him. She tightened her grip on the railing.

"Are you all right?" he asked.

She looked at him, helpless, haunted by a love she hadn't asked for, hadn't known how to handle, by a passion that wouldn't leave her completely.

A shock of dark hair, a whispered voice behind her at the theater, a graceful movement of a man glimpsed at a distance and it was like a door opening inside her, welcoming the man whose image the hair, the voice or the movement had invoked.

"Yes," she said, gathering herself together. "Of course. I thought I'd check in with you to let you know I was in town."

"What are your plans?"

"Well, I have to pick up the key to the house I rented—"

"I have it. The agent left on a fishing trip. He said he might not make it back if the fish were biting, so he gave me the key last Friday."

"Oh. Well, good." What else was there to say? Her residence while she was here could hardly be kept a secret. "I want to go out to the site where the bones were found as soon as possible."

"Right." He sounded crisp and official. "You have a meeting with the tribal chairman and attorney in the morning. They want to discuss the situation."

"Okay." She could tell Judd didn't like the idea of consulting with the others. If a crime had been committed in the county, he wanted to jump right on the case.

He was a man who took his responsibilities seriously. When they'd suspected she was pregnant that summer many years ago, he'd insisted they marry immediately. "Growing up is hard enough in this day and age without being a bastard in the bargain," he'd said, then grinned. "I don't intend to let you go."

She knew his own youth had been unhappy. His parents, though married and wealthy, had quarreled all the time. When Judd had come out to Montana on a vacation after practicing law with his father for three years, he'd liked the wide, open spaces, the peace he'd found there. That was the summer they'd met.

He'd stayed—against his parents' wishes—and started work as a rookie in the sheriff's department when they married. They'd been deliriously happy that year. At least, she had.

"We'll go to the site after the meeting. You'll need to wear jeans and hiking shoes. It's rough country." He looked at his watch. "Have you had lunch?"

"No, I'd forgotten about it."

He nodded and looked away. "Yeah."

Tracy knew he was recalling the past. He used to tease her about losing herself in whatever she was doing, whether researching forensic techniques or planting a garden. He'd often arrived home to find her buried in a project, no supper on the table, the bed unmade, in spite of her good intentions.

He would always chuckle at her consternation, and they would end up making love. Later, they would prepare the meal together.

Judd had been a patient, forbearing husband. Eight years her senior, he'd been indulgent toward her enthusiastic rush through life. He'd made no demands, except that she welcome his caress....

She turned her back on him and the memories he invoked and headed for her car.

"We'll go by your...house first. Then we'll pick up something to eat and go to my office. I have the reports you requested and the topography maps," he said, easily keeping up with her, his stride long and surefooted.

She wondered at the hesitation before he mentioned her rental house. Was it because he, too, remembered the house they'd built together? It had been small but per-

fect, set on its own ten acres with woods all around it, next
to Route 17.

After the divorce, the house had been sold and the profit
split between them. She'd invested her share, unable to
bring herself to spend it. It had felt like blood money,
spoils from the death of their marriage...and the death of
their son.

Judd pulled out of the parking lot in his unmarked
county vehicle, which was a black sports utility truck. The
only difference between it and others of its kind was the
wire-mesh glass that could be rolled up between the driver
and the rear seat, and the fact that the rear doors couldn't
be opened from inside the vehicle.

Behind him, Tracy eased into the traffic flow and followed him to Pale Bluff Lane. The rental house was a
white, two-bedroom cottage set behind a picket fence.
Multiflora roses covered the fence along the side of the
driveway.

He stopped in front of the house while Tracy turned into
the drive and parked under the carport. He met her at the
front door, fished the key out of his pocket and let her
precede him into the house. "I, uh, had someone come
over and give it a good cleaning on Saturday. It was rather
grimy."

"Thank you." She was clearly startled by this news. She
looked around the tiny living room. "Oh, this is really
nice." Her smile was hesitant, but pleased.

He noticed the way the light from the window reflected
in her eyes, turning them from mossy to golden green.
He'd liked to make love to her outside, on the grass with
the sun streaming over them, her eyes the color of new
leaves as she smiled up at him.

When they'd made love like that, he'd carefully shielded her tender skin from the sun with his own body, which tanned easily.

He cursed silently at himself. "I'll bring your stuff in."

"I'll help," she said. "It isn't much."

It wasn't—only a soft-sided suitcase with wheels and a nylon carpetbag with a matching makeup bag. He recognized the latter. She'd asked for them as a Christmas present years ago. He and Thadd had picked them out. He was surprised she still had them, or that she would use them.

But then, two years ago he had repurchased the house they'd shared as man and wife. He wasn't sure why, except it was the only place he'd ever been truly happy. He wondered if she knew....

He doubted she'd ever wanted to know about him after she left town. She'd left the state *and* the country after the divorce.

For a second, the emptiness threatened to fill with the black grief of those days. He trampled it down roughly. Emotion had no place in his life, not anymore.

He suddenly remembered a time from the past. Tracy had turned on him in anger. "Tell me how to stop feeling!" she'd cried. "Our son is dead. Tell me how to stop hurting!"

He'd had no answers for her, no words of comfort. He hadn't wanted to talk about it. The pain was too much. He'd walked out.

Later, knowing he'd failed her, he'd tried to hold her, to make love and erase the bitter hurt, but she'd pushed him away, coldly rejecting him. In that instant it had become clear that she blamed him for their son's death.

He blamed himself. He was the one who'd laughed at her fears. He was the one who'd encouraged Thadd to roam the woods, to watch for animals, to learn the ways of nature.

Their son had been shot through the lungs from a quarter-mile distance with a high-powered rifle. The police had never found whoever had fired the shot. It was doubtful the hunter had even known he'd hit anything, much less an eight-year-old boy tracking a deer.

"That's all," she said. "Judd?"

He blinked, then nodded, pulling himself from the past as if walking across land mines. He willed the emptiness into place.

Carrying the suitcase and carpetbag, he followed her back to the house and into one of the two bedrooms. It looked a hell of a lot better than it had on Friday when, out of curiosity, he'd come over to check the place before Tracy arrived.

At that time the floors, windows, curtains and furniture had been dusty and stained from the last people who'd rented it. Judd had called his cleaning woman for help. Mrs. Johnstone and her son had dashed to the rescue.

It had taken the three of them all day Saturday, but the cottage showed the results in sparkling windows, sweet-smelling curtains, shampooed rugs and furniture and scrubbed floors.

Outside, the son had mowed the yard while Judd had weeded and clipped back the roses. Together they had washed the windows, then the doors and window facings smudged with fingerprints.

A sense of satisfaction hit him. At least the cottage wasn't a disappointment to her.

"Just set them down anywhere," she told him. "I'll freshen up and be with you in a minute."

"Take your time. Change to something more comfortable if you like. We're still casual here in the country." He didn't know why he'd added that little barb. It was just that she looked so damned sophisticated...so damned *untouchable*...in that silk suit.

He placed the luggage on the bed and hurriedly departed. The bed, covered in a white frilly spread with gold-and-pink poppies embroidered all over it, was giving him ideas.

He paced to the back door and gripped the framing as he looked at the clear vista beyond the yard.

Pale Bluff Lane ran across the lip of a limestone outcropping that formed a bluff rising twenty to fifty feet above the lower part of the valley floor, where Highway 191 curved north and ran the length of the county.

His county. His domain and responsibility.

He leaned against the jamb and crossed his arms over his chest, worry forming inside him. Tracy would be officially in charge, but it was going to be his case.

A murder investigation was no place for a woman as delicate as Tracy. Hell, she'd been squeamish over the wild game he and Thadd had brought in for dinner during various hunting seasons.

Actually, it might not be a murder case. That was what she was supposed to tell them. The department needed the who, what, why, where and when of the bones found on the reservation before they would know if they had a case.

"Okay, I'm ready," she said from behind him.

He turned and stopped stone-still. She had changed into slacks that matched the golden yellow suit, but had retained the printed blouse and suit jacket. Her hair was drawn back from her face with a barrette, and she wore tasseled loafers.

She looked like the girl of nineteen he'd first seen on a rarely used hiking trail, watching him drink before he plunged into the cold pool to bathe.

At that time she'd been dressed in jeans, a yellow T-shirt and a long-sleeved, yellow-checked shirt open down the front. She'd driven him to instant arousal then. She did the same now.

"God help me," he muttered, and forced himself to walk out the door before he did the same thing he'd done two weeks after that first meeting—kiss her until she was pliant in his arms.

Tracy nibbled on the chicken sandwich without much enthusiasm. Judd had gone to a fast-food place out on the highway. Now they sat on opposite sides of the desk in his office while he filled her in on the case.

"Last March, George Sweetwater found the bones—"

"George," Tracy interrupted. "I remember him. What was he doing in the woods, especially in that area? It's sacred ground."

"He says he was running his dogs to keep them in trim for the hunting season in the fall."

Tracy had to smile. "He was rabbit hunting," she concluded.

Judd's eyes met hers. He smiled, too. "Out of season," he added. "And without a license."

"He doesn't need a license on tribal ground."

Tracy knew tribal law better than most of the Cheyenne. She had spent every summer since her earliest years on the reservation, helping her father gather oral histories and myths about the tribe.

As a history professor at the university, he'd made Montana Native Americans and pioneers his particular field. He'd been delighted when his daughter had followed in his footsteps—sort of—with her degree in anthropology. That was before she'd gone into forensic science.

"So you're still up on local codes," Judd remarked dryly.

"I reviewed the case with my father."

"How is he?"

"His knee is bothering him some, but he stills walks up the hill every day." She laughed, thinking of the steep hill overlooking the campus in Missoula. "Faster than some of his students. In fact, he loves to challenge the freshman history class to meet him at the top for their first lesson."

Judd's deep chuckle rippled over her, setting up vibrations in some molten inner core that she rarely acknowledged. She wanted no soft, vulnerable places inside her. She didn't want to respond to him in any way.

"I'm sorry about your mother," he said, the smile fading.

Tracy's mother had died in an accident two years ago. Her father had been lonely after that. "Thank you. And your folks?"

"They're fine. My niece graduated from high school."

"Oh, yes. She's eighteen. I'd forgotten."

The cooling breeze from the air conditioner swirled a strand of hair across her mouth. She pushed it back, then refastened the clip that held the thick waves away from her face.

When she finished, she glanced across the desk and caught Judd watching her. The harsh expression on his face stunned her.

Then it was gone, and she wasn't certain what she'd seen. But there for a second, as he'd watched her fix her hair, his expression had been so grim, she thought he must hate her.

"Anyway, George found the bones near a bluff. Apparently someone from the reservation called the FBI before my department was notified," he said, a note of irritation visible when he balled the hamburger wrapper in his fist. He gathered his debris and stuffed it in the white paper bag.

She quickly ate the last of her sandwich and spicy french fries. "Did you examine the bones?"

He snorted. "Are you kidding? I got a glimpse of them, but the tribal police won't let anyone near them. Sara Lewis—you remember her?"

Tracy nodded. She could vaguely remember the younger woman.

"She's curator of the Native American Museum here in Whitehorn," he continued. "She and some of the tribe think the bones belong to some long-lost ancestors of theirs."

"They might," Tracy reminded him mildly.

He grimaced in disbelief. "Are you ready to look at the officer's reports?"

She nodded. The cool air sighed over her face, a soft, slow caress like that of a lover. She recoiled from the idea.

She'd known some of the old feelings and memories were bound to be stirred by her return to Whitehorn. She just hadn't realized they would be so strong.

But he'd always done that to her, she admitted.

Judd had always made her think of touching and loving and all those other things associated with the male-female attraction from the very first moment they had met. It came as a shock to her that he still did. And that no other man ever had.

While she read the field reports of the people who had made the initial investigation after George had brought the bones into the tribal-police office, Judd returned several telephone calls.

She noted his tone seemed different with other people compared to the one he used with her. When he talked with the mayor, the tension she'd heard earlier was gone. In its place was a relaxed amusement with a sincere undertone—Judd took his responsibilities seriously—as they discussed plans for the county fair scheduled for the next weekend.

When his secretary, Juliet Clarke, came in with some letters for him to sign, Tracy felt a strange jolt of some peculiar emotion, sort of the way she'd felt when she witnessed the caress Maris Wyler had given him.

Judd and the attractive blonde talked quietly. His voice held a lazy resonance that shivered right down Tracy's spine. He had a way of listening while seeming to stare at the ground or off into space, then looking at the speaker with a slow, sideways glance, his full attention on the person.

It was very appealing to a woman to be the center of that attention, which had a dark, sensual aspect to it that Tracy didn't think Judd even knew about.

Women did. They fell at his feet like trees in the path of a tornado.

When he finished with the letters and the secretary left, he placed another call. He laughed after identifying himself. The other person must have said something very humorous. Tracy thought it was a woman's voice on the other end of the line.

She tried hard not to listen, but Judd's laughter rumbled over her like distant thunder, vibrating right down to her toes. She clenched the report. Against her will, she wondered if he was talking to Maris. He was making plans for the evening.

When he hung up, she laid the brief reports on his desk. "I'd like to see the topos now."

He removed the topography maps from a cabinet and spread them over the cleared surface of the desk. Moving around until he stood beside her, he stretched his arms wide as he opened the rolled map.

"Hold that corner," he requested.

When she did, he used his left hand to point out the location of the crime scene...if there had been a crime. Bones did not necessarily mean murder and mayhem. They might even belong to an animal instead of a person.

His shoulder pressed against hers as she leaned forward to study the area. A jolt of sensation shot through her. She moved slightly away and sensed his quick look.

When she glanced at him, she witnessed a harshness that hadn't been present when he'd talked to his date for the evening. She stood very still as a storm of emotion swept her in its path.

The moment stretched...became forever....

The secretary knocked and stuck her head in the open doorway. "Sterling is on line two."

Judd moved back around the desk.

Tracy breathed once more. "I have all the information I need. I think I'll go home."

He paused with his hand on the telephone. "I'll drive you in a minute."

"Uh, no, I'd rather walk." She picked up her purse and slipped out of the office. She knew she was running away. She just didn't know from what.

Two

Tracy explored the town before starting home. She compared the stores and buildings with her memories. Some things had changed. Some had not.

Mason's jewelry store had had an antique clock in the window seventeen years ago when she and Judd had married. It had been there when she'd left town seven years ago. It was there still. However, the name on the sign indicated the son was now the jeweler. She assumed the older Mason had retired.

A new supermarket occupied a corner, but she couldn't recall what had been there before it. She walked to the house, drove back in the rental car and bought groceries.

The sun was beginning to set when she returned to the cottage. The sky was gilded in shades of rose, gold and lavender when she finished putting her groceries away and arranging the kitchen. She unpacked the clothing she'd brought.

Sitting at the table, drinking a cold soda, she listened to the sigh of the wind through the pines. The only sound in the house was the steady *drip-drip* of the faucet.

She tried to turn it off and failed. She made a mental note to pick up a washer at the hardware store and replace the worn one.

After that, she changed from her good clothes into old, much-worn jeans, a blue T-shirt and a nylon Windbreaker with blue sleeves and interesting splashes of primary colors on the rest. She thought of eating, but decided she wasn't hungry.

Leaving the house, she wandered across the backyard to the rocky outcropping that overlooked the highway down below. Cars whipped past fairly steadily. It wasn't like city or freeway traffic in California, where she now lived, but the road was busy for a small town in southern Montana.

Yellowstone traffic, she decided. Families on vacation, going to see Old Faithful geyser, or maybe they'd already been to the park and were heading on up to the Lewis and Clark National Forest to camp and fish.

She leaned against a tree and gave a shaky sigh. Darkness seemed to fill her soul. She'd talked with a psychologist a couple of years ago. The woman had told her she needed to face the past and come to terms with her grief before she could get on with her life. Tracy had thought the doctor crazy.

Now she wasn't so sure. Returning was harder than she'd expected. Emotions she'd buried in her work were stirring, and she couldn't seem to stop them.

She spotted a vehicle on the highway that reminded her of Judd's unmarked sports truck. Was he with his date now? Did he take her to his place after dinner? Or did he go to hers? Was he getting on with his life as the doctor had told her to do?

Tracy squeezed her eyes tightly shut, unable to bear the thought of him making love to another woman.

She felt lost and confused and unable to cope.

All this on the first day back in town, she mused, trying to mock her emotions. She trembled to think of the coming days with Judd. He would want to be in on every detail of her investigation.

Maybe she could solve the case quickly and go back to where it was safe. In California, they only had earthquakes, mud slides and wildfires to deal with.

Restless, she walked north along the bluff. The sky was an interesting watercolor of lavender fading into blue fading into deep purple-blue. When the path angled back to the lane, she followed it without question.

Almost in a trance she turned left on Silver Creek Road, then right on Stoney Ridge. In another few minutes, she stood in front of the rustic rail fence along the front of the house she and Judd had built. Honesty forced her to admit he'd done most of the work, but she'd loved helping.

They had worked so hard that fall, getting the outside done so they could finish the inside during the winter. Later, it had been nip and tuck to see which occurred first—completing the house or having the child that spring.

Judd had put the final touches on the nursery three weeks before Thadd had been born.

She gripped the log railing with both hands as she stared at the house. It had natural stone halfway up the sides, then split redwood logs the rest of the way. Wide, double-paned windows framed views of the woods on all sides.

The steep pitch of the roof allowed two rooms upstairs, one as a guest bedroom, the other for storage of all the treasures families collected and couldn't bear to throw out.

She wondered if the same family lived there. No one seemed to be home. There were no lights inside that she could detect.

Walking along the fence, she stopped by the front gate, which stood open. A red-and-white soccer ball lay by the road. She picked it up and studied it as if she'd never seen one before.

Finally, her chest tight and achy, she tossed the ball gently toward the house so that it came to rest by the two steps leading down from the front porch. She thrust her hands into her pockets and quickly walked down the street.

Instead of returning home, she headed for the main part of town. She realized she was hungry.

Crossing the street, she went to the Hip Hop Café. The small eating place hadn't been there eight years ago. It wouldn't bring back any painful memories. She pushed open the door and went in.

The café was a jumble of used tables and chairs that were bright and colorful. The place had a vibrant charm that must make it popular—along with its good food, going by the delicious aromas. A jukebox sat in a corner. Two samplers decorated the walls, among various other things. The first person she saw was Lily Mae Wheeler, widow, divorcée, town gossip. Tracy hesitated, but it was too late to turn around and skedaddle back to the cottage.

"Well, bless my soul! Would you look what the cat dragged in?" Lily Mae demanded of no one in particular. "Tracy Hensley."

When Lily Mae pushed out a chair with her three-inch-spike heeled sandal, Tracy had no choice but to join her.

"When did you get into town, hon?"

"Today. Around noon," Tracy answered.

"I'd heard you were coming—oh, here's my dinner." She picked up her purse to make room for the dinner plate. "Melissa, were you in town when Tracy lived here? About five, six years ago, wasn't it, Tracy?"

Since Lily Mae didn't leave anyone time to answer questions, Tracy and the other woman spoke at once.

"It was seven years ago when I left—"

"I wasn't here then—"

They both stopped, then smiled at each other. Lily Mae broke right in. "Melissa Avery, this is Tracy Hensley."

"Roper," Tracy corrected. "Tracy Roper. I decided to use my maiden name after the divorce."

Melissa frowned thoughtfully. "I remember. You were married to the sheriff. Your little boy..." She trailed off, embarrassed at bringing up the subject.

"It's all right," Tracy said quickly. "I'm glad to meet you."

"Tracy is a famous FBI agent," Lily Mae put in.

Melissa expressed an interest in what she did.

"Actually, I'm a consultant on special cases," Tracy explained. "I also work at archeology digs as an anthropologist for the University of California sometimes, although forensic investigations are taking more of my time."

"I'm fascinated," Melissa told her, "but I have to get back to work. We're shorthanded tonight, so I'm helping wait tables. I'll bring you a menu in a sec." She hurried away.

"You two should be friends," Lily Mae announced. "You're both hardworking and independent as hell. Now tell me what you've been doing since I saw your father last spring."

Tracy told Lily Mae of her doings after she ordered a salad special. It was nice to know some people never changed, she mused while they ate and talked. The gay divorcée had once had an eye for Dr. Roper, but he had seen no one but his wife.

Tracy worried briefly over him getting hooked now by the voluptuous woman, who preferred to call herself a widow.

Maybe that wouldn't be so bad. Her father, a workaholic like herself, had buried himself in his book project this past year.

Lily Mae, with her bleached hair, outrageous earrings, loud laughter and come-hither glances, might be good for him. She was good-hearted, and might introduce some fun into his life—a spark of unpredictability. Heaven knew, one could never tell what the woman would say or do next.

Tracy controlled an urge to giggle at the idea of staid Professor Roper being tugged through life by Lily Mae.

"So I told her she should try spanking his bottom and that would put a stop to those tantrums," Lily Mae said, ending another story while Tracy finished her meal. The hoop earrings with two-inch parrots sitting in the hoops swung to and fro.

Lily Mae was in her fifties. She'd never had children, and her marriages hadn't lasted all that long.

Tracy realized the woman was lonely. She'd adopted the residents of the town and county as her extended family, thus she felt quite free to give out advice on any subject to anyone. A wry affection warmed Tracy's heart for the talkative widow.

"I guess you heard about Maris Wyler, didn't you?" Lily Mae asked over fresh blackberry cobbler and ice cream.

Tracy's heart leapt to her throat. "Maris?" she said cautiously. She didn't want to hear of an engagement. It was none of her business what Judd did in his private life, but... she didn't want to hear about it.

"She up and married some drifter that came through, a rodeo rider just like that good-for-nothing husband of hers who got himself killed. The man showed up claiming Ray had died owing him some money. Which was probably true."

"So... Maris is married to—to this other man?"

The parrots swung wildly as Lily Mae nodded. "She just had a baby a few months ago—his name is Clay. I always thought Maris had a head on her shoulders, but you know what passion can do to a person."

Tracy felt a rush of heat to her face. She bent over her cobbler and scooped up the last bites. When she looked up, Lily Mae was studying her curiously.

"She and Judd went out some for a year or more, but nothing ever came of it. Sometimes a person can't get over that first love. Your father is that kind, I think."

A flash of mutual understanding passed between them. Tracy touched Lily Mae's hand in sympathy. The widow, for all her bright clothes, jewelry and painted face, had more depth to her than appeared on the surface.

During the rest of the meal, they chatted about the town and its various problems. It was dark and surprisingly late when Tracy refused a ride from Lily Mae and started home.

As she passed the mayor's house, she heard the familiar gravelly rumble of a deep voice. She ducked her head and tried to hurry. She didn't want to see Judd and his date saying good-night to the mayor and his wife.

"Tracy," he called out before she could get more than three-fourths of the way past the mansion.

She stopped and turned. Judd stood alone on the paved driveway next to the house. He was dressed in a suit and tie. Her heart knocked hard against her ribs.

"Hello," she managed to say in a nonchalant voice. She looked at him, then away.

His face wore a frown when he came to her at the end of the sweeping drive. "What are you doing out after dark?"

She bristled at his tone. "Is there a curfew you didn't tell me about?"

That brought him up short. "Of course not," he said in a more reasonable manner. "It's just...it's after nine. Not many people wander around a small town this late."

She didn't owe him an explanation, but she found herself giving one anyway. "I went to the café for dinner. Lily Mae Wheeler was there—"

His muted groan brought a stop to the words. "Say no more. She talked your ear off for three hours."

"Well, two," Tracy admitted.

"Get in. I'll drive you home." He motioned to a low-slung sporty-looking car at the curb.

"This is yours?"

"Yeah."

His direct gaze challenged her to make something of it. They had never been able to afford a new car, much less a luxury vehicle such as this, during their marriage, but they had teased each other about the one they would buy "when our ship comes in."

The plans they had made...so many dreams and hopes...so many bright promises for the future...

"Trace?" he said, shortening her name as he used to. He held the car door open for her.

She got in, feeling very uncertain about the wisdom of this. She hadn't felt this self-conscious the first time they'd made love, there on a grassy meadow with the June sun pouring over their entwined bodies.

It took less than five minutes to get to her house. He sat in the car after turning off the engine. "You didn't leave the porch light on."

"Uh, no. I didn't expect to be gone so long. I mean, I was just out for a walk. I'd thought I might go to town for dinner, but I wasn't sure." She stopped the incoherent chatter.

For some reason, it was more difficult to talk to him knowing he wasn't involved with Maris.

That didn't mean he wasn't involved with someone else.

She realized it must have been the mayor's wife on the phone earlier that day, inviting him to dinner. Tracy wondered if there had been an extra woman at the table for him. She shied away from the thought. It was none of her business.

"Look," he said harshly, "I don't know if we can work together if you're going to act as if you suspect my motives every time I speak to you."

"I don't know what you mean."

"Don't you?" he snapped. He swung his head around to glare at her in the dim glow cast by a streetlight on the corner. "Admit you didn't want me to come to the house this morning. Admit you didn't want to have lunch with me. Hell, you didn't want to come into my office to review the case."

"Judd—"

"Do you hate me that much?"

She gasped, stunned by the question. "I—I don't hate you at all." She stumbled over her denial.

He faced forward, staring out into the darkness behind the cottage. Trees were visible as a darker outline against the dark sky. A sliver of moon hung above their branches.

When he said nothing more, she ventured, "All right. I admit I was reluctant to see you. I think having a few misgivings would be the natural order of things, considering our past. It was bound to be awkward...this first meeting. It brought back memories."

"Yes," he said. "God, yes."

The silence, the dark, the close confinement of the sports car crept over her like a warm cape.

"You'd better go in," he said.

She didn't want to go into the house, not alone. She didn't think she could bear the silence.

Besides, she felt they might be on the verge of discovering something important about each other and about their time together before. Perhaps it *was* time she faced the past. "Would you like some coffee?" she heard herself ask.

He frowned as if he were going to refuse, then nodded. When he climbed out, she did the same. He removed his jacket and tie and tossed them onto the seat. They went into the dark house.

"You should leave some lights on when you go out," he told her. "A lamp on an electronic timer is a good idea."

"I will." She turned on lights as they made their way to the kitchen. Once there, she started a pot of coffee. She noticed her hands were trembling when she stripped off her Windbreaker.

"Coffee cake?" she offered.

"No, thanks. I had dessert at the mayor's house. He's already started his goodwill campaign to win reelection." The irony in Judd's tone made her smile.

"Is anyone thinking of running against him?"

"Not that I know of."

"What about you?"

"What about me?" He gave her a puzzled glance, his expression once more guarded.

"You'd make a good mayor. You're well known for your honesty. You get along with the city council."

He gave an amused snort. "I don't like the kind of politicking it takes to get elected. Even as sheriff, I find I can't always say exactly what I think."

"Yes, you're a man of few words," she said wryly.

She considered this statement. Judd *had* been a quiet man, especially about his feelings. Perhaps she should have pushed him to talk to her. Perhaps she should have made him listen when she'd wanted to explain her feelings. Perhaps... But it was too late now. As the Cheyenne said, the path of life is a one-way road.

She poured the coffee and took it to the table. He held her chair for her. He'd always been gallant. It was one of the things that had attracted her to him from the first. He was gentle with women and children, at ease with his fellow men.

When his hand brushed her shoulder, she felt a leap in her pulse rate. It was scary, the things he could still make her feel, or was that part of once having been as close as earth and air?

He sat opposite her. They drank the steaming coffee. He opened his shirt collar and rolled his sleeves back. She tried to think of something innocuous to discuss, but nothing came to mind. She wanted him, she realized.

"Why did you come back?" he asked suddenly. He sounded angry. "Why now, after all this time?"

She swallowed as emotion gathered in her throat. They'd met in June. Seventeen years...

"Frank Many Horses asked for me," she finally said. "He wanted someone who would understand tribal ways and respect their ancestors and their customs."

He studied her, as if wondering whether this was the truth, his dark gaze so penetrating it made her wonder at her decision to accept the case. Since she worked as a special agent, on a consulting basis only, she could have refused.

"I saw your father last summer," Judd mentioned. "He said you were buried in your work. He was worried about you."

This was news to her. "Why?" she asked in surprise.

"He thought you didn't have a life outside of your studies. He said you didn't go out much."

"Oh." She licked her lips. Her mouth seemed to have dried up. Little sensations spiraled off inside her. "Well, I have been busy. However, I do see friends occasionally."

"Friends?" Judd questioned. His gaze seemed sharper.

"I do go out," she said firmly. "Some."

The clock in the living room ticked off the seconds as he silently absorbed this information.

Judd knew he should leave. It was dangerous to stay here in this quiet house with Tracy. She was the only female he'd ever met who could make him forget his good intentions. Hell, she made him forget the basic instincts of self-preservation.

"Some," he repeated, hot anger going through him at the thought of the men who might have touched her. He fought the rising hunger in himself, the conviction someplace inside him that this woman belonged to him.

Not anymore, he reminded himself ruthlessly. Somehow that bright flaming passion had used itself up, like the fuel of the sun, burning itself out in a fury of intense heat.

A man would be a fool to trust those feelings again. When he'd first seen her, some gut instinct had said she was his. He'd believed it then; he knew better now.

He stood abruptly.

She did, too.

Her green eyes widened as she gazed into his. He knew what she saw. She'd always been able to read him like the front page of a newspaper when it came to passion. He cursed himself for wanting her, for thinking he needed her. He didn't.

He didn't need anyone. Hadn't the last seven years proven that—eight if he counted the final, devastating year of their marriage before it fell apart? "I'd better go."

She nodded.

Neither of them moved.

Her lips parted as if she would speak, but she didn't.

He moved toward her. "One day," he murmured. "One day, and I already wonder what you would taste like, how you would react to my touch if we were to kiss."

"I—I...me, too."

Her confession threw him further off balance. He'd expected her to deny the attraction. He'd wanted her to. Now the admission lingered in the air between them like gunpowder that might explode at any moment.

Slowly, he reached out. He almost wished she would disappear, the way a mirage would when a person tried to grab it.

She didn't vanish.

Instead, with a sigh, she settled into his arms when he enclosed her in an embrace. Some part of him wondered what he was doing. An experiment, he decided. It was an experiment. But he had no idea what he was trying to prove.

And then it didn't matter. His lips met hers. She made a little choked sound in her throat. He held her tighter.

The kiss burned through him, driving out everything but the need for her, fed by eight long years of starvation.

She moved her head from side to side, as if trying to deny the kiss. He slipped his hands into her hair, which felt cool on the surface, but was warm, so warm, underneath. He held her face up to his. She stopped the restless movement and stared at him.

"You mustn't," she whispered.

"Don't tell me no," he growled. It wasn't what he wanted to hear from her. He wanted acquiescence, acceptance...*response*.

Tracy thought she might faint, she was so light-headed. When he framed her face with his long, sensuous fingers, she felt the tremor in them and was afraid for both of them.

They were becoming enmeshed in something neither could control. She knew she should push him away, but her hands spread over his chest. The warmth of his skin under the white shirt radiated into her cold fingers.

It seemed she'd been cold a long time.

"No," she said, but it was a whimper of need.

His hands tugged at her T-shirt, pulling it from her jeans. Then they slipped under the material and caressed her back. His hands were large compared to her slenderness. They felt strong and capable on her flesh. And gentle . . . so gentle.

She'd instinctively trusted him and his touch from the first moment they'd met. It was like that all over again.

"Touch me," he growled low in her ear, his mouth raining hot kisses all over her face.

She obeyed mindlessly, reaching for the shirt buttons, opening them, pushing his shirt aside so she could reach the bare flesh underneath. She pressed her nose into the rough diamond of wiry hairs on his chest and inhaled deeply.

Judd groaned helplessly. When she touched her lips to his chest, the caress was as hot as a branding iron. He wrapped his arms around her, lifting her from the floor, bringing her into searing contact from lips to chest to stomach to thighs.

He placed her on the counter. She opened her legs, letting him come close, tacitly giving him permission to explore further, whether she knew it or not.

His heart leapt like a jackhammer in his chest, and for the briefest second he wondered what he was doing. And then her tongue touched his nipple, causing flames to shoot through him, burning out all other thoughts.

Tracy felt the spasm that went through Judd and experienced the wild thrill of triumph. He still went crazy in her arms. As she did in his.

He pushed her T-shirt up and unfastened her bra. The cool night air hit her breasts, then was gone, shut out by his hands as he cupped her against his palms.

His lips sought hers when she lifted her head. She saw his eyes close, felt his breath blow across her mouth, and then his mouth was on hers, demanding, exploring, seeking the passion that she'd thought was dead.

She felt his hands move, pulling his shirt free, brushing it to either side, then the controlled weight of his chest settled against hers. Flesh against flesh. Hot and wonderful and wild.

A throb started between her thighs as the hard length of his arousal pressed there. He moved against her, again . . . and again.

Once during the embrace—after a minute or an aeon, she wasn't sure which—he said her name against her mouth, and his lips trembled on hers before he slipped his tongue inside.

The smooth thrust of it was a wanton replay of the many times their bodies had plunged together until she'd cried out in ecstasy.

A moan tore its way out of her, from deep inside where she was vulnerable, where emptiness demanded fulfillment, where love dwelled, all alone and in darkness.

She turned her head, her breath panting from her body. She was afraid to feel this passion, afraid of what feelings might come after. . . .

"Trace," he said.

There was no choice. She had to look at him.

He shook his head, and she knew he, too, was fighting the needs that drove them. She looked away.

He eased her bra into place, his hands shaking as badly as hers, and pulled her T-shirt down over her bare skin. Then he fastened his shirt.

"I'm sorry," he said.

That surprised her. "It was both of us," she insisted, taking her share of the blame.

She put her hands on the counter, preparing to jump down. He caught her by the waist and lifted her, setting her on her feet and making sure she was steady before he let her go.

"You're shaking," he said. "So am I."

He gave a snort of laughter. The bitterness of it cut into her. She didn't know what to say. Everything was confused.

"We overreacted to the tension," she finally offered by way of explanation. It was the best she could come up with.

"Tension? That's a new name for it."

She pressed her fingertips to her temples, where a headache now throbbed mercilessly. "Don't," she pleaded. "Let's forget it happened. It's late, and we were... our defenses were down."

He spun away from her. "Why the hell does it have to be you?" he demanded. He tucked his shirt into his dress slacks.

The harshness had returned to his face, and he looked ready to destroy something. With a low curse, he reached out and twisted the faucet handle. The steady dripping stopped.

The inane thought came to her that she probably wouldn't be able to turn it back on.

"I'll fix it," Judd said. He looked around the kitchen, but apparently didn't see anything to vent his fury on. He rubbed a hand over his face and pressed his fingers against his eyes.

Tracy realized how very tired and vulnerable he looked. She felt the same. Her throat was tight and achy now. She feared she might cry at any moment. She swallowed a couple of times. The feeling passed, but the terrible sorrow lingered inside her. She felt sorry for both of them.

"I'm going now." He dropped his hand from his eyes and studied her. "Will you be all right?"

"Yes."

"Maybe we'll solve the case soon, and you can leave."

She nodded, too weary to answer. They walked to the door.

He paused before going out into the night. "I'm sorry," he murmured again, so low the words might have been the sighing of the wind.

Three

Judd held the door for her the next morning when he came by. She climbed into the truck. He didn't touch her. She was grateful for that. They were both subdued, careful of each other. It was just as well. They had to maintain a distance.

During the night she had made up her mind to ignore the storm signals between her and Judd. She wasn't nineteen anymore. She could control herself. After all, she'd had no trouble doing so in the presence of some very attractive men in California.

After a few minutes of stilted conversation they gave up talking. Tracy watched the passing scenery. In less than an hour they arrived at the reservation. Judd drove along the main road to the tribal headquarters.

At the council offices, they went inside and were directed to the conference room. A carved wooden box sat on the conference table. Sara Lewis, who, according to Judd, worked at the Native American Museum, stood on the other side of the table.

Tracy smiled and nodded to the younger woman, who returned her greeting cautiously.

A few elders of the tribe stood around to observe what would take place. At the end of the room was the tribal chairman, Frank Many Horses. The attorney, Jackson Hawk, also a tribal leader, was with him.

"Jackson!" Tracy exclaimed in pleased surprise. He was the same age as she was. They had played together when they'd both been free of the demands of education—she from public school in Missoula, he from the BIA boarding school he'd been forced to attend. "I heard you had returned."

Jackson was as tall as Judd. His hair and eyes were black as obsidian. He wore braids tied with rawhide strips which to her looked perfectly natural with his suit and tie. His jutting nose and prominent cheekbones proclaimed his Cheyenne ancestry.

He'd gone to college on a basketball scholarship and earned his law degree after that. His lithe body proved his athletic skill; his alert gaze indicated his mental acuity.

The attorney came to her, his smile bright and warm. His welcome lifted her spirits, which needed all the help they could get, she admitted ruefully.

"Tracy, daughter of the professor who goes around asking personal questions," he teased. His smile disappeared. "Now you're here to ask your own questions."

"Yes. Do you have the bones?"

He nodded. "My uncle wishes to speak with you."

Jackson took her arm and led her to the old man, who stood at the back of the room by the council table. Judd fell into step behind them. Tracy noted the way his gaze darted from her to Jackson, as if he were assessing the situation between them.

The tribal attorney introduced her to Uncle Frank as if she hadn't known the old man all her life.

She stood quietly, waiting for him to speak. When he did, she realized he was much older than he'd seemed the last time she had talked to him. A second heart attack had taken away some of the inner strength she had always associated with him.

The thought made her sad, as if a way of life would go with the passing of the man.

"How are you?" he asked.

"Fine."

"Your father?"

"He sends you greetings. He has to finish the book with the new oral histories this summer. He'll bring you a copy, he said."

The thick brows, almost white now, pulled together. "Good," he said. "That's good." He looked around as if tired.

A young tribal policeman pulled a chair into position. "Here, Uncle," he said, using the honorary title. "You must rest. Dr. Hunter said we were to make sure you do."

"Kane," the elder snorted. "He's an old woman."

Tracy saw the old man was pleased at the care.

When he was seated, he motioned for the young man to bring a chair for her. When she faced him, their chairs placed so that their knees almost touched, he spoke again. "Kane needs to find a wife, as his cousin has had the good fortune to do." He looked at his nephew in affection.

"Jackson?" Tracy inquired.

"Yes. Just last week." The attorney smiled. For a second she glimpsed the quiet joy in his eyes. He gestured toward his uncle. "He's turned into a matchmaker in his old age."

Her eyes were drawn to where Judd had taken up a position against the wall while he waited for the greetings to be over and for them to get down to real business. She couldn't tell if he was impatient with the proceedings or merely resigned.

"I wish you happiness," she said softly.

Jackson nodded his thanks.

"You know the story of the bones?" Uncle Frank asked.

She waited a few seconds before answering in order to give the question and her response the consideration they deserved. Her summers on the reservation had taught her it wasn't polite to jump into speech without prior thought.

"I've been told a little. Would you tell me again so that I may have the facts clear in my mind?"

Uncle Frank recounted the story she had learned from the initial report to the FBI and from Judd. The sequence of events was the same. After the tribal elder fell silent, she thanked him. She waited, then asked to see the evidence.

"It isn't proper for the remains of ancestors to be despoiled by the white methods," he said, giving her a frown that would have sent her scurrying if she'd still been a child.

"The forensic investigation," Jackson clarified.

Tracy gazed at the floor while she reflected on this. "No test will be undertaken without tribal permission," she promised.

Nearby, she felt the movement as Judd stirred in surprise at this rescinding of authority. She touched her finger to her lips to bid him be silent, then faced the tribal chairman squarely.

Uncle Frank studied her until she thought he was searching out every lie she'd ever spoken. He nodded.

A wave of relief swept over her. She wasn't going to have to be the pushy representative of the federal government.

"Now come and let us talk heart-to-heart," Uncle Frank said, standing and opening his arms. She went into them for a warm hug that had her fighting the sting of tears all of a sudden. "You and Jackson begged many a treat of fry bread and honey at my house when you were young. You'll come soon and share a meal with us?"

"I'd love to."

There was some chatter now in the background. She glanced at Judd. He was more impassive than the most stereotyped Indian in any movie she'd ever seen.

She and the tribal elder talked about her career since she'd left town years ago. She'd finished her master's degree and done field work with the world's foremost forensic anthropologist for three years, traveling all over the world.

"This living with old bones doesn't bother you?" Uncle Frank inquired over coffee. The box on the table wasn't referred to during the conversation.

"No. I find it fascinating to try and figure out ancient people's lives—how they might have lived, what they did for food and medicines." She paused. "How they died."

He nodded and sat silently for a long minute. "Jackson, open the box," he said.

Tracy felt a beat of excitement. Finding old bones was like a treasure hunt for her. She loved to study the past.

Because it was safer?

She ignored the inner question and went to the table. Jackson slid the box in front of her. He unlocked it, then carefully lifted the top off. The silence in the room was that of a held breath. She looked inside while the handsome attorney laid the top to one side.

The first thing that caught her eye was a deep scratch in one of the bones, which were the skeletal remains of an arm and part of a hand. The scratch gleamed white against the brown-stained surface surrounding it.

She glanced behind her, to where Judd still leaned against the wall. His mouth relaxed just a bit, not enough to call it a smile. Jackson's tightened as the three exchanged glances that admitted what the two men had suspected from the first.

"These aren't old bones," she said.

* * *

The truck jolted over a road that grew increasingly rougher. Tracy grasped the door handle and the seat edge in an effort to keep from bouncing.

When the road became a logging or hunting trail winding upward through some thick woods, Judd slowed down.

It didn't take a forensic expert to know he was in a foul mood. He hadn't spoken two words since they'd left the council house and started for the site where the bones had been found.

The road ended abruptly near a bluff—a limestone-and-shale cliff ranging from ten to a hundred feet high, with the Beartooth Creek running at its base.

The creek separated the Kincaid ranch from the reservation, ending in Lovers Lake on the ranch. It was near the lake that she had first seen Judd that summer long ago.

She brushed the thought impatiently from her mind. She had a job to do. She leaned forward to change from her sandals to socks and hiking shoes.

The land angled steeply upward from the small open meadow where they stopped. The trees and brush were thicker in the section on the other side of the clearing, she noted.

The sacred woods. Uncle Frank had given her permission to explore the area.

Judd parked beside a tribal police car and a marked sheriff's-department truck. Tracy jumped out before Judd could come around to help her.

Hooking her purse strap over her shoulder, she headed toward the bright yellow police tape attached to the trees. Judd caught her by the elbow.

"This way," he said. He let her go and started off at an angle to the road. He ducked under the tape and held it up for her, his face expressionless as he waited.

She quickly followed, irritated at his cool assumption of authority. "I want to circle the site before homing in on the place the bones were found."

That's the way forensic investigations were conducted—start at the outer perimeter and spiral in. Leave the site by retracing the same path. That way the investigator ran the least risk of ruining the evidence, if any was present and assuming it hadn't already been trampled by others who'd been there before her. Judd knew this as well as she.

"That's what we're doing," he said tersely. He let her take the lead, but directed her by voice as they walked the site.

She examined the lay of the land, the types of vegetation and the rock formations as they worked their way to the bluff, then up along its spine and finally down into the center of the woods. They met a tribal policeman and a deputy from Judd's department there.

Judd introduced her to the two men. She spoke briefly to them, her gaze going to the marked area in the dirt. Moving carefully, she circled the small yellow flags attached to stiff wires pushed into the ground. She finally stopped and stooped to inspect the bones uncovered in the dirt.

"George Sweetwater took the bones he found from the site. Those were the ones you saw at the council house," Judd explained, dropping to his haunches on the opposite side of the markers. "We found the tribal police going over the area when we got here. They had discovered the rest of the bones belonging to the hand—"

"How do you know these belong to the bones in the box?"

"It was an assumption," he said curtly.

She nodded and continued to study the site. She could tell it grated on Judd to be fighting over a motley bunch of bones like two opposing packs of dogs. He was also stifled in getting on with the investigation by the impasse with the tribal council.

It wasn't like him to let his temper show, though. At least, it wasn't like the man she'd once known.

During the years of their marriage, she'd rarely seen him let his emotions get the better of him, not even at their son's funeral. Neither had she.

In the face of his stoicism, she'd held her grief inside. Sometimes she'd wondered if they might not have made it if they'd cried in each other's arms.

Last night, after he'd left, she'd felt like crying, although she hadn't. That episode in his arms had been an aberration on both their parts, she decided, one driven by passion, not emotion.

She sighed, stood and studied the rising slope above them.

Judd did, too. "Plenty of shrubs and plants around," he said, following her thoughts. "Bones couldn't wash down here all of a sudden because of erosion."

"They've been brought here, probably by animals. The question is where were they to begin with...and how long have these pieces been in the woods?"

"Yeah."

"Has the site been photographed?" she asked.

"Yes. We have a full set of prints at the office."

"Well, let's pack up the evidence and see what else we can find. By the way, do you have an office I can work out of? I promised Uncle Frank the bones would be kept in a secure place. I'm not sure the cottage would qualify."

"There's a small conference room next to my office. You can use it if you like." He smiled grimly. "The department will bill the FBI for rent and phone use."

"Rent?" she demanded in disbelief. "For an unused room?"

"I didn't say it was never used. All right, no rent," he conceded when she started to argue. "But you pay for your long-distance calls."

"Agreed." She smiled, feeling relieved. They had established a working relationship. That was good. If they could keep their dealings strictly on a business level, all would be well.

And if they didn't?

She ignored the question. While Judd supervised the other two in gathering and sealing the evidence, she walked the area again, keeping to the same perimeter.

Tomorrow, she decided, she would widen the search pattern until she found the rest of the skeleton or had to give up. Two weeks were all she'd planned for this case.

"Are you about through? I'm ready to lock up."

Tracy looked up from the table where the evidence was laid out on white paper. She laid the magnifying glass down. "Yes. I've noted every chip and scrape on these. The gouges were caused by animal teeth, as I thought. Tomorrow I'll start a systematic search of the area."

Judd frowned. She prepared herself for an argument.

"I'll assign someone to assist you."

"I'd rather you didn't."

"You're not going to wander around in the woods by yourself," he informed her. "Someone was murdered there."

"We don't know that," she said calmly.

He glared at her. She glared back.

After a couple of seconds, his lips relaxed slightly at the corners. "You're a stubborn cuss," he muttered.

She was reminded of times past. Their quarrels had never lasted for more than a few minutes. One or the other of them would start laughing at the stubborn look on the other's face, then they'd end up making love, or scooping Thadd up and going out for ice cream.

"I know." She smiled at him, then stretched her stiff muscles and yawned. "I'm going home. What time will you come in tomorrow?"

"Seven." He bent over the table and studied the small collection of bones.

She noticed the silver hairs threaded through the black locks—not many, but some.

Gray hair? Judd?

To her, he was the quintessential man, never aging, never changing, an archetype who served as the model for all the men she'd ever met. To observe signs that he was as vulnerable to aging as the rest of humanity disturbed her.

Not for the first time she wondered if she'd expected too much from this strong, silent man.

"What time will you arrive?" he asked, straightening and glancing at her in that sultry, devastating manner he was so unconscious of.

"The same as you."

Ignoring the lifting of his eyebrows that questioned her early arrival—she tended to be a night owl—she cast an eye over the small conference room to see if there was anything she'd forgotten to do. Everything was in order.

Picking up her purse and the hiking shoes she'd worn at the site on the reservation, she exited through Judd's office.

Judd locked the conference-room door, then followed her to the outer office. His secretary had gone home for the day.

Tracy started down the broad hall while Judd locked the office door.

"Do you want to go to dinner?" he called after her.

She stopped and glanced over her shoulder at him. "No, thanks. I thought I would visit Winona tonight. I called her earlier today. She's expecting me."

He nodded.

She rushed along the hall and out into the warm air. She drove to the cottage and changed clothes, replacing her slacks with a pair of white shorts dotted with blue-and-yellow butterflies, putting on the matching knit top and grabbing her Windbreaker for when the sun went down.

In ten minutes, she was speeding along Route 17. A few miles from town she pulled off the road into what looked like a junkyard—and in reality was.

The sign that proclaimed the place to be the Stop 'n' Swap was barely legible. It swung from a signpost at an angle, one side an inch higher than the other due to the uneven lengths of chain that held it in place.

Below that sign was another that said wild honey was made and sold on the premises.

The entire front yard was filled with discarded household and auto items. Birds flitted around a feeder. A dozen cats snoozed in the sun. Two goats stood on top of a rusted station wagon and eyed Tracy as she parked by the open gate. The watchdog, an old blue tick hound, didn't raise an eyelid at her approach.

An eagerness to see the old woman she loved nearly as much as her own family propelled Tracy from the car, past an old bathtub filled with dirt and planted with moss roses and up to the door of the trailer where Winona Cobb lived. Winona stood in the door.

"Tracy!" she exclaimed warmly. She held the screen door open.

Tracy leapt up the concrete blocks that formed the steps and a small porch. She was enveloped in a hug.

Winona looked just the same—the same gray hair braided and wrapped around her head, a round, merry face with brown eyes sparkling with intelligence and wry wit, a short, rotund body that was sturdy and stout.

She'd put on a long flowered skirt and a faded blue blouse for the occasion, but she'd forgotten her shoes. Around her neck and dangling from her ears she wore polished stone beads and crystals of various colors.

To Tracy, she looked like an aging hippy. Most outsiders, upon meeting her, assumed she was one of the Northern Cheyenne. No one knew for sure where she'd come from, and Winona never told. Like the hills, she'd been part of the landscape forever.

Tracy and her father had visited frequently during their summer trips to the area. The old woman had served homemade wine and lemonade and sent them home with bags of fresh vegetables that she grew in a huge garden beside the trailer.

"Well, child, let me look at you," she said, moving back from Tracy, who was half-a-head taller. She clasped both Tracy's hands and studied her with a fond smile.

All at once an alarmed expression flitted over the lined face. Winona dropped Tracy's hands as if they'd burnt her. She crossed her arms over her chest and staggered back.

Blindly she reached out, found a chair and sank into it. She clutched the beaded necklace in a trembling hand.

"Winona?" Tracy said in alarm. She dropped to her haunches beside the padded rocker.

"Two faces," Winona murmured, her eyes closed, her tanned face going pale. "One woman...two faces." She shook her head slowly from side to side.

Tracy's heart was thumping. She'd forgotten about Winona's visions. The woman was a known psychic. She'd been the one who'd told Judd where to find Thadd when they were searching for him. Tracy didn't discount anything she said.

"Can you see anything else?" she asked quietly.

"A room. There's a man on a bed. Naked. He's asleep. The woman is looking for something...she's going through his pockets...."

Tracy waited, but her old friend said nothing more.

Winona opened her eyes. She put a hand to her head. "Bring me a glass of blackberry wine, then put on a pot of chamomile tea."

Tracy did as she was told. She kept a keen eye on the older woman to make sure she didn't go into another trance and maybe choke on the wine. When the tea was ready, she prepared two cups and laced them generously with wild honey.

"Are you all right now?" she asked, pulling up the footstool where she'd loved to sit and listen to Winona's stories of bygone times for hours on end. She placed the cups on the end table and helped herself to a tiny glass of homemade wine.

"Yes. Who did you last touch before you came out here?" Winona asked after taking a swallow of the sweet, potent wine.

Tracy took a sip and let it roll over her tongue. She thought about her day. After returning to town from the reservation, she'd spent the afternoon in Judd's private conference room, poring over the bones.

"I haven't touched anyone since Frank Many Horses...no, I shook hands with Jackson Hawk when I left the res."

She tried to recall if she and Judd had touched. They hadn't. They'd both been very careful around each other all day. In fact, he'd left the office after showing her the room she could use and hadn't returned until shortly before five.

"That's all that I can remember," she finished. "Do you recall what you said?"

Winona nodded. "A woman with two faces. One over the other. I could see them both, but I couldn't tell who either was. It was one of the strangest visions I've ever had."

"You looked frightened."

"Not me. It was her...them. There was only one body. But two faces." Winona sighed and sipped the wine, slower this time. "I sensed she was angry...very angry...but also scared."

A frisson caused Tracy to draw her arms tightly to her sides. Winona's vision gave her a chill. "You think the vision came from me?" she asked, trying to find some clue to its meaning.

"Oh, yes," Winona said. She looked suddenly worried. "I just got another bit."

The hair crawled on Tracy's neck. "What?" she asked.

"You might...I think...there could be danger." She frowned and closed her eyes. After the silence stretched into a full minute, she shook her head. "It's gone. But I sense danger."

"Well, perhaps more will come later. Do you feel like showing me your garden? I loved those little cherry tomatoes you grew when I was a kid. And the sweet basil. It was like perfume to me."

After she admired the vegetables, especially the pumpkins and squash, they chose a big watermelon and cut it from the vine. Tracy carried it to the back of the trailer.

Natural stones formed a patio there. An oak tree provided shade over a picnic table. A line of stubby cedars formed a windbreak on the north side of the yard. The place was an oasis of flowers and fruit trees, as peaceful and pleasing as the front yard was cluttered and utterly disordered from Winona's trade.

They switched to iced tea with their meal, which was mostly vegetables, fresh bread and cheese made from the nanny goat's milk.

The goats, cats and hound joined them on the patio, but politely kept their distance. Winona didn't let them intrude on guests. Bees buzzed lazily among the flowers.

After polishing off big slices of watermelon for dessert, the two of them sat on lounge chairs and chatted. Winona called a cat to her and let it sit on her lap. Slowly she stroked its orange fur while the sun set in a brilliant display of fiery red. Tracy played with a black-and-white kitten.

"Tell me of your life," Winona ordered gently.

Tracy told of her travels and studies. "You wouldn't believe all the things a bit of research can tell about people nowadays, even those who lived thousands of years ago. I'll probably have to run a DNA check on the bones from the reservation."

"The tribal elders won't like that," Winona predicted without having to resort to psychic abilities.

Tracy wrinkled her nose. "They've made that clear. I promised I'd not do anything without their permission. Judd didn't like *that*. I'm going to search the area thoroughly first. I'd say by the depth of the dirt stains, the bones haven't been in the ground for more than twenty or thirty years. There should be other evidence. Of course, nature can fool you sometimes. I could be wrong."

She chatted on, drawn out by alert questions from her listener. Vaguely, she realized she hadn't talked to anyone like this in years, not since she and Judd used to plan their future.

"What is it?" Winona asked.

"What?"

"You had a thought that made you sad."

Tracy stared at the lined face. She sighed and took a drink of the spicy tea before answering. "It's hard...to come back to the place where all your dreams died."

"Are they truly dead?" Winona asked in a kind voice.

Tracy sifted through her memories. "Yes."

"But there are new beginnings. You're too young to give up on life."

"Well, I haven't." Tracy laughed, albeit a bit shakily. She pinched her forearm lightly. "Ouch! See? I'm still living."

Winona smiled at her foolishness. "Aren't there any men in California who have taken your fancy?"

Tracy's laughter faded. She stroked the kitten, which had curled into a ball in her lap. Its purr vibrated through her body. She suddenly felt the terrible ache of loneliness.

"No," she admitted. "I've dated some, but..."

"But they're not your true love."

Tracy pushed a strand of hair out of her eyes with an impatient gesture. She gazed into the distance, where night gathered behind the mountains to the west of the wide valley. The clouds had dried up during the night and no longer wreathed the far peaks. "Were you ever in love, Winona?"

"Everyone is in love at some stage of life."

"What was he like?" Tracy sat up straighter, curious about this woman's life. "Were you married?"

"No. He was a poet. He loved me, but he loved the world more. He went away to discover his Muse." She studied Tracy for a short spell before continuing. "He came back—I lived in the city then and taught English at the local college—but I was angry with him and sent him away. I regretted it afterward."

"Did you ever see him again?"

Winona nodded. She carefully smoothed the cat's fur. "Twenty years later, he returned. We were in our forties. Neither of us had married. He said he had to see me one more time. We lived together for a month. He died in my arms."

Tracy thought it the saddest story she'd ever heard. "I'm so terribly sorry."

"A month of memories isn't a lot to take a person through a lifetime...nor are a few years. The nights get lonely."

They sat in silence, each lost in thought.

"Well," Tracy said at last, "I suppose I should get home. I'm so glad I came. My father and I miss our summers here and the visits with you. He sends his love."

A smile lighted Winona's face. "I hear he may be getting married any day."

Tracy was startled. "Who to?"

"Lily Mae." The merry brown eyes twinkled. "She told everyone at the café she was going to nab him when he came back to town. She said two years was long enough to grieve."

Tracy didn't know whether to be amused or offended. "Dad won't be down this summer, but perhaps I'd better warn him of the widow lying in wait."

"Let him find out for himself," Winona advised. "Getting caught by Lily Mae isn't the worst thing that could happen to a man. She might be good for him."

"Funny, I thought the same thing when she and I were talking last night. Did you somehow listen in on the conversation?"

"My ability doesn't run to eavesdropping, although I sometimes wish it did."

They walked around the trailer to the front. The last dying rays from the sun lighted the western horizon to a paler blue than the rest of the sky, which was a deep royal blue.

"Have you missed the country since you've been gone?"

Tracy did a slow turn, looking in all the directions of the compass like a Cheyenne saying his prayers.

To the south of them, the Beartooth Highway ran over the high pass. The land dropped off a thousand or more feet on each side of the crest where the cars crawled along the narrow, winding drive. Most travelers found the Beartooth Pass a heart grabber.

To the west, Crazy Peak rose over eleven thousand feet. The Beartooth Creek ran east out of the mountains into the reservoir that gave Whitehorn its water supply. North and east of town the land was flat to rolling, not as rugged, but with its own beauty.

"Yes," she admitted.

"You must move back."

Tracy looked at her friend. "I can't."

"You will," Winona said with absolute conviction.

Four

Tracy walked the path to the site, her sneakers making no noise on the mossy ground under the thick stand of trees. Behind her, Sterling McCallum—Judd's top detective, according to the secretary—walked along, equally silent.

Judd and Sterling made a good pair, Tracy thought sourly. Neither spoke unless absolutely necessary. Sterling was helping her search the site for clues. Judd had told her Sterling was his best man for the search, that he had a "good eye."

She carried a paintbrush and dustpan, a pick, rock hammer and chisel, all tools of the archeological trade. She was going to dig for treasure . . . or in this case, bones.

No one was at the original location. The tribal elders had given her permission to do whatever she had to do. She set her tools out, tossed a cushion on the ground and plopped down.

Leaning over, she surveyed the ground where the other bones had been found. She formed a square with wire posts and string and began removing the top layer of dirt and leaf mold. No other site in her surveys had yielded so much as a clue, other than this one.

An afternoon of digging yielded the rest of the finger bones. She placed them in evidence bags with tweezers and wrote the location on a piece of paper and stuck it in the bag. She then recorded the information in her log book.

"You're good," McCallum said when she finally packed up her finds and indicated she was ready to leave.

"Thanks."

She gave him a curious glance as they returned to the police vehicle they'd come out in. He hadn't helped with the dig at all. Instead, he'd wandered around the area, peering at first one thing and then another as if he had nothing particular on his mind.

Once she'd seen him picking thimbleberries off a bush and eating them. He'd brought her a handful. She'd been grateful, for she'd forgotten to bring a water canteen with her.

She paused at the ridge and looked over the flat grassland below. "What are those?" she asked, pointing at some strange animals near the creek.

"Beefalo," McCallum said.

"Ah. I thought they were the strangest-looking cows I ever saw." She smiled. "A melding of the old and the new. I wonder if it will work."

He shrugged. He was a big man—big hands, big feet...a big heart? Hard to tell, but he *had* brought her the berries to munch on. He looked tough and had a military bearing. She was sure his nose had been broken at least once.

He wore a silver-and-turquoise ring and a wedding band. There had been some teasing banter between him and Judd that morning about the last big case he'd been assigned to...something about an abandoned baby. Apparently he and his wife had adopted the infant last fall.

Tracy couldn't imagine those large hands being gentle enough to hold a baby. But then, Judd had been incredibly wonderful with Thadd, even when the baby was a newborn and had weighed in at seven pounds, two ounces.

Her heart gave a squeeze, and she dropped that line of thought. Instead, she concentrated on what she'd learned during the past week. With tribal permission, she'd sent a small section of bone off to the forensic lab in California. When she got the results, she'd know how long the bones had been there.

On the way back to town, she decided to have a showdown with Judd. For three days—Wednesday, Thursday and today—he'd sent whatever policeman he could spare to stay with her at the site. She didn't need a baby-sitter, and she was going to tell him so.

"You like digging up bones?" McCallum asked.

"Yes." In her mind, she was rehearsing what she was going to say to Judd.

"How'd you get interested in that?"

She frowned at him. "What?"

"Never mind," he said. "I can see you're thinking of other things." He grinned, a slow, lazy smile that reminded her of Judd.

There seemed to be an understanding between the two men. They were kindred spirits, she decided. They shared certain, intangible characteristics...like being quietly stubborn when she'd insisted she didn't want anyone tagging along with her.

Pity the man's poor wife if McCallum were as much of a watchdog as Judd was proving to be, she thought waspishly.

When they arrived in town, the detective let her out at the police station and drove off. She carried the loot up to her assigned room. Judd had given her a key to his office, but she didn't need it. He was in, talking on the telephone when she went through.

She realized he had put her right where he wanted her. He or his secretary could keep on eye on her comings and goings with no problem whatsoever. She gave him a withering glance and sailed on by, closing the door after her.

Opening the bag, she laid out the new finds and compared the bones to the original ones George had found and to the bones found by the tribal police. They all fit together.

From the size of the hand, she assumed the person had been a male, twenty to forty years old. That was a rough guess. The hipbone was best for information on the sex and age of the person.

Getting out her magnifying glass, she studied all the bones for signs of breaks or thickening at certain places that could indicate the type of work he'd done. Bone density and wrist size indicated whether the person had been left- or right-handed.

Provided she ever found the other hand to compare the two.

The door opened. "How's it going?" Judd asked.

She laid the glass in its case. "Fine. I found some more bits." She glared at him. "While your watchdog stood around bored as all get-out."

The dark eyebrows jutted upward. "You sound tired."

"I sound irritated," she corrected. "Don't get in the way of my investigation, Judd. I'm ordering you to back off."

The tension in the small room escalated to tornado-warning velocity. Since the passionate episode, they'd stepped around each other with the caution of two cats who'd arrived in a new and strange territory at the same time.

But, she reminded herself, she was the top cat. And he'd better not forget it.

"All right. You're on your own." He spread his hands as if he were giving up. "The fair opened today. Winona called and wanted to know if you were going. She's entered several of the food categories, and they're being judged this evening. She wants to have supper at the fair afterward."

"I'll call her," Tracy murmured, the heat taken out of her anger by his cool acceptance of her authority.

She arranged to meet Winona at the main gate at six. She glanced at her watch after she hung up. It was already after five.

If she wanted a shower and change of clothes, she'd better get with it. She covered her work and laid her tool case on the end of the table. After clipping on her waist purse, she started out at a brisk walk.

Judd wasn't in his office when she left. She told the secretary good-night.

She'd left her car at the cottage, since it was as easy to commute on foot as by vehicle in the snug little town. On impulse, she walked around by the house she and Judd had built.

Strange, but she never saw a family there. In fact, she never saw signs that anyone lived there at all—no lights in the house, no car in the garage . . . well, the garage was always closed, but surely they'd leave the door open once in a while.

However, the place was well kept up. The yard was mowed and weeded regularly. The rock garden she'd designed looked nice. She and Judd had planned it so very little maintenance was needed.

They both had liked the natural look of shrubs and pine needles and rocks, forming curving walkways among the many trees.

She rushed by and went on to her cottage. After a quick shower, she slipped on her favorite gold slacks and a gold silk shell with a white-and-gold-striped linen jacket for evening.

The gold loops she wore in her ears and the matching bracelet had been a gift from her father one Christmas years ago.

She glanced at the clock. Five to six. She considered, then decided her waist purse was the handiest to use. It left her hands free, yet kept her money and wallet right in front of her where she could keep an eye on them.

The county fairgrounds were five miles south of town. She arrived at ten after six, parked and dashed to the entrance. Judd was there, talking to an attractive woman.

It wasn't Maris Wyler—or whatever her name was, now that she'd married—but another woman who wasn't at all like Maris.

This woman looked very delicate. Her manner was demure. When she laughed and glanced up at Judd, then quickly away, she seemed shy.

And very attractive. A Laura Ashley type in a floral print skirt with a white lacy blouse and a bow holding her hair at the back of her neck.

Tracy felt a return of that odd emotion she'd experienced when she saw Maris pat Judd's cheek on Monday. Before she had time to define it, Judd saw her. His smile disappeared like spilled milk among farm cats.

She went forward, her shoulders squared as if going into battle. She forced herself to relax and smile calmly.

Judd made the introductions. "Mary Jo, this is Tracy Roper. Tracy, Mary Jo Kincaid."

Tracy shook hands with Little Bo Peep, as she named her in her mind, disliking the sweetly feminine woman on sight. Which wasn't at all fair or nice, but...

"Oh, you must be the FBI agent," Mary Jo exclaimed in a soft, almost breathless voice. "I just can't imagine doing dangerous work like that." She gave a delicate shiver and leaned against Judd's arm as if seeking protection.

"Dead people aren't dangerous," Tracy said bluntly. "Only the living." She ignored the ominous frown Judd gave her.

Tracy tried to place the woman. She knew the Kincaids fairly well. She and her father had collected their pioneer stories and read their great-great-great-grandmother's diary of the trip west. There had been two sons, one of which was dead. She didn't remember any daughters.

"Mary Jo was the children's librarian here. She and Dugin Kincaid were married last June."

"Oh." Tracy noticed the diamond rings on Mary Jo's left hand. A feeling like relief washed over her. Her smile became genuine. "I hope you'll be very happy."

"Oh, I am. Dugin is just wonderful to me. Well, I've got to go. I'm supposed to judge flower arrangements in a few minutes. It was nice meeting you." She hurried off toward the gate, leaving a trail of expensive perfume to mingle with the scent of popcorn and hot dogs from a nearby stand.

Tracy glanced up to see Judd watching her with a definite look of hostility in his dark eyes. "Yes?" she said.

"Mary Jo has had a hard time this past year. First an abandoned baby was found on her fiancé's doorstep, then the body of a stranger was discovered during her wedding. And her father-in-law died two months ago. Jeremiah was a strong man and losing him turned the family upside down. Mary Jo is shy and doesn't open up to people easily. I thought you might be friends."

Tracy fumed at his censorious tone. "Why should she need me when she has *you* for her champion?" she asked acidly.

His eyebrows lowered like a thunderstorm about to start.

Tracy backed up a couple of steps. "I have to find Winona."

"She's at the vegetable-judging pavilion. She said to meet her there," he told her. He reached into his shirt pocket. "Here's your ticket." He handed it to her.

He, too, had changed clothes before coming to the fair. In jeans and cowboy boots, with a red shirt and denim jacket, he was incredibly attractive. He wore a Wind River hat, gray with a gray-and-black woven band. Not showy, but seductive just the same.

Her heart seemed to be beating against her ribs all of a sudden. Jealousy, she thought. She was jealous of any woman he smiled at. She swallowed and tried to ignore the painful beat.

"Who do I owe for it?" she asked, taking the ticket.

He looked annoyed. "No one. I had a couple of free passes." His smile was sardonic. "Perks of the office."

"Well, thanks." She paused, not sure what to do. "I'd better meet Winona." She hurried off without waiting for a reply.

Judd let her go. He watched her long, slender legs striding purposefully toward the gate. She handed over the ticket, got her hand stamped and went inside.

She couldn't get away from him fast enough.

He snorted cynically. Since that episode in the cottage, she stayed a cautious distance from him, as if she thought he couldn't be trusted around her.

He couldn't. That's what made him mad as hell. And another thing—he'd been flirting with Mary Jo, on purpose, knowing he was doing it and knowing that Tracy could see them talking while she crossed the parking lot and approached them.

His skin seemed too small for his body all at once, as if filling with needs too long denied. A clamoring hunger in him was growing and pushing to be let out. He clamped down on the unwanted desire. Not Tracy. No way. Never again.

Shaking his head, he walked more slowly toward the entrance. Winona had asked him to eat with her and Tracy. He didn't want to.

Tracy stirred up too much... tension in him. Yeah, his libido was real tense when she was around. He smiled grimly at the joke, but didn't find it all that funny.

Tracy saw Winona standing by an arrangement of gourds and pumpkins on a tray. The fall decorative display had a red ribbon for second place on it.

"Is this yours?" she asked. "It's lovely. Congratulations on the ribbon."

"It's only second place," Winona said grumpily. "I'm glad to see you. I'm hungry enough to eat a bear, hide and all." She smiled and reached over to straighten an ear of Indian corn.

Her hand brushed against Tracy's.

Tracy heard the gasp, then felt Winona sway. She put an arm around her. "Winona? What is it? Are you ill?" She wasn't sure if the psychic was having a vision or a heart attack.

"Rocks," Winona whispered, leaning heavily against Tracy, nearly making her stagger. "No, one rock...coming down hard...falling...falling...anger...furious anger..."

Tracy felt a strong arm slip under hers. Judd took Winona's weight easily and held the rotund body close until the spell was done. Their eyes met over the shorter woman's head.

"I have her," Judd said in a soft rumble.

Tracy caught Winona's hand in hers and rubbed gently.

Winona pulled away as if hurt. Her eyes snapped open. "Who have you touched?" she asked in a weak tone.

Tracy shook her head. "It must have been the bones. I found more of them this afternoon."

Winona nodded. She seemed to be okay.

"What did you see?" Judd asked.

"It was strange," Winona told him, her expression once more serene. "There was a rock, hitting something... or someone... I couldn't tell about that. Just this rock, flying through the air and hitting, then hitting again, only downward this time."

"Hmm."

The two women waited while Judd thought about it.

"The bones," he said to Tracy. "Maybe it was murder, after all." He turned back to Winona. "If you get any more visions, I want to know about them, no matter how remotely connected you think they are or how odd."

"All right. Now, about some supper."

Tracy noticed Winona didn't point out her second-place win to Judd. It came to her that the woman had a small streak of vanity of her own. She smiled and walked with the two back to the hot-dog stand.

The incident was forgotten as the three of them got their meal and found a table. The detective, Sterling McCallum, and his wife were in the food line behind them. Tracy knew Jessica Larson McCallum from before. Her father had tried to help Thadd when he was found. The couple was pushing a lovely, happy baby in a stroller. She looked eager to explore the world. Tracy smiled though she couldn't help remember another child so eager for adventure. Judd invited them to join him, Winona and Tracy at their table.

"Two women," McCallum mused after he and his wife sat down and introductions were made. "How do you rate that, Boss?"

"Just lucky," Judd said with that lazy grin that caused a shaft of longing to go through Tracy. When he shifted his chair to make room for the couple, his arm brushed hers.

"Don't get any ideas," Jessica McCallum told her husband. "You have enough going with the two women you've already got!" She took Jennifer out of the stroller and handed the toddler to her husband.

He cradled his daughter in one arm. She looked up at him and nestled sleepily. He smiled and tweaked a lock of her hair, but Tracy saw the tenderness in his eyes as he glanced from his daughter to his wife. She recognized the look of a man who was well satisfied with his lot in life. The tough detective had two soft spots, it seemed.

Tracy was touched by their happiness. Her gaze met Judd's. He looked at her so intently that she became flustered. She squeezed her hot dog. Mustard flew out the end and landed on her silk top.

"Here," Judd said. He picked up a napkin and dipped it in a cup of water. He slipped his fingers under the edge of the silk shell and rubbed the spot. His efforts only made it worse.

"Try spit. It might take most of it out," Winona advised.

Judd moistened the napkin with his tongue and went back to work.

Tracy felt the heat radiating from his hand into her flesh. Although he hardly touched her and his hand was a respectable distance from her breast, she kept getting hard, stabbing jolts of electricity all the way down her torso.

Her breath became jerky. In fact, her lungs were hardly working at all. She could feel sweat popping out on her forehead. "Don't."

Her protest apparently didn't register with him. He wore a frown of intense concentration as he worked on the stubborn spot.

When the tip of her breast clenched into a tight bead, perfectly visible under her bra and top, she grew desperate.

"Stop!" she said, the word coming out as a shrill cry.

Everyone stopped what they were doing and stared at her and Judd. His long fingers were still inserted under the edge of her blouse as he, too, went still. For a long second, they sat frozen into place.

She wished she could sink out of sight right into the ground.

A brick red flush swept up Judd's face. He released her blouse as if it were a hot coal.

"I think that's as good as you're going to get it," Jessica announced. She deftly changed the subject. "Sterling said you found some more bones today. Did they go with the others?"

Tracy was grateful for the new topic. "Uh, yes. I feel sure we'll find more. It looks very promising."

The conversation became general after that. Later, she and Judd went with the McCallums to the rides while Winona spotted Lily Mae Wheeler and went to talk to her. They all tried the Ferris wheel, then paused by the carousel.

Tracy was totally surprised by Jessica McCallum. She teased her husband unmercifully. "I'd like to ride the merry-go-round, but the horses will probably run off when they see you coming."

"I promise not to sit on one," he shot right back. "Although I might sit on you before the evening is over if you keep up the wise remarks." He gave her a menacing scowl that didn't frighten her in the least.

He bought five tickets and handed two to Judd. Judd looked at Tracy with a question in his eyes. She drew a deep breath and got in line behind the other couple. Judd stood behind her.

It was with trepidation that Tracy stepped up on the carousel platform. Jennifer chose a blue horse with a silver mane. Sterling lifted Jessica up on it so that she and their daughter sat sidesaddle. He stood beside them, his arms placed protectively on either side of his women. Jennifer laughed but waved at everyone.

"Let's take a swan boat," Tracy suggested.

Judd nodded.

They climbed in and sat on the wooden bench. In front of them, two girls, about nine, squealed with delight as they leapt upon two unicorns, which were white, with golden horns projecting from their foreheads.

"Beautiful mythical creatures," Judd remarked as the music speeded up and they started turning.

"Yes."

He had taken her to a carnival in July, nearly seventeen years ago to the day, a few weeks after they'd met. They had been on the merry-go-round when she'd suddenly become nauseated. He'd swept her off the unicorn she'd been riding and signaled the man to stop. In the privacy of his car, when she felt better, he'd questioned her gently. They had realized she was most likely pregnant.

"I should have taken better care of you," he'd blamed himself.

He'd gone with her to face her parents and tell them they wanted to be married right away. Six weeks after they'd met, they were married. Their son had been born in March.

For nine years, the marriage had been good.

Then one autumn a freak accident had destroyed their happiness. They had lived in the same house another year, but it wasn't the same. Unable to bear the mockery their lives had become, she'd asked for a divorce. Judd had moved out of the house while the legal arrangements were made. When the divorce was final, she'd left town, never intending to return.

The merry-go-round completed one full turn and started another. She thought of life, going around and around. Going nowhere, it sometimes seemed. That was her life.

Ahead of them, Tracy saw Sterling lean over and listen to something his daughter babbled. He laughed. Jessica kissed him on the cheek. He turned her face with a finger under her chin and claimed a quick kiss on the lips before tousling Jennifer's curls.

The tenderness between the other couple caused an ache to start deep inside Tracy. Once, she'd had that.

When she looked at Judd, he was staring off into the darkening sky, his jaw set in a hard line. Anger, raw and hurting, roiled in her. She wanted life to be different. She wanted all it had promised those many years ago. She wanted to start over....

Clenching her hands together, she forced her thoughts away from those lines. It didn't matter what she wanted. Life couldn't be lived over and adjusted to suit one's idea of happiness.

She would never hold another child in her arms. After Thadd's birth, she'd had a severe infection that had left her barren. She and Judd hadn't been able to conceive another child, although they'd both wanted a brother or sister for their son.

Judd touched her hands. He gently pulled them apart and held her right hand, rubbing it between both of his. "Don't think on it," he murmured soothingly. "Let it go, Trace."

Gradually, the feelings subsided, and she felt only the ever-present tinge of sorrow that colored her days. She stared at Judd in wonder. The harshness was gone from his eyes, and he looked at her in...pity?

She pulled her hand away. She didn't need pity from anyone. What had happened had happened. A person had to go on. She knew that. She was getting on with her life.

Was she?

Yes.

"I'm all right," she assured him. She smiled to show him. After the ride, she said good-night to the McCallums, having decided to return to Winona and talk to her for a while before returning to the cottage.

Lily Mae and several others sat at a large table where they'd left the older woman. The widow, wearing three-inch-long blue-and-purple earrings that matched her colorful knit pants and top, introduced Tracy to everyone and told her something of each person's life. "Tracy is the FBI expert investigating the murder on the reservation," she finished.

"Murder has not been established," Tracy hastily corrected.

"Well, everyone knows that's what happened," Lily Mae asserted with an authoritative air. "Why else would a skeleton be there?"

"People die of lots of things," Judd said, coming to stand beside Tracy. "A woman choked on a hot dog last week down in Big Timber and was nearly asphyxiated before the medics got it out."

Lily Mae peered at her hot dog, then shrugged. "There are worse ways to go." She finished off the last bite while the other women laughed or looked shocked, according to the way they viewed Lily Mae and her outrageous quips.

Tracy smiled. Maybe she'd have her father down next weekend for a home-cooked meal and invite the widow-divorcée, too. Her eyes went to Judd. No, she wouldn't invite him.

"Winona, I think I'll go home now," she said. "How would you like to go out to dinner tomorrow night? I thought I'd try the new pizza place I saw near the library."

"That sounds fine. I'll come by your house around six."

"Good. Well, good night. It was nice meeting all of you." She smiled at the group, then headed for her car.

Judd accompanied her. "It's dark," he said when she glanced at him. "A woman shouldn't be in the parking lot alone."

"I'm sure no crook would dare impose on your territory."

He lifted one black eyebrow at her mocking tone. "The fair brings in a lot of strangers."

They walked past the rows of cars. He was right, she realized. A dark parking lot was a lonely place. "How do people like Lily Mae come up with so much gossip, or in this case, the truth?"

"You have evidence of murder?"

"No." She paused at her car. "But Winona's vision—that rock hitting someone. I think she's seeing something connected with the bones. It's happened twice now, both times after I've handled the evidence. I think our mysterious victim was killed by getting bashed with a rock."

Judd drummed his fingers on the top of her car. "Well, if a rock did it, there's no shortage of weapons in the area.

Or the county.'' He nudged a half-buried rock in the hard ground of the parking lot with the toe of his boot.

Tracy yawned. She hadn't been sleeping well that week. Maybe tonight she'd get a proper rest without waking and lying in bed for hours, thinking of the past.

''Judd, thank you for earlier. When we were on the carousel,'' she added when he looked at her questioningly.

His expression turned grim. He stared out into the night. It came to her that there was a blackness in his soul that matched the one in hers. Once there'd been such joy between them....

''It's hard not to remember,'' he said in a low tone.

''I know.''

Sympathy stirred in her. Life could be unbearably hard for a man of Judd's temperament. He was a man of action, a person who got things done. But even he hadn't been able to save their son. Like her, he could only wait, pacing the hospital corridor while the doctor operated.

She climbed into her car, said good-night to him and drove off. Looking in her rearview mirror, she felt a wrenching pain inside as she observed him watching her drive off. If things had worked out differently, they would have been going home together.

Five

Tracy woke to bright sunlight streaming across her pillow. She'd slept fitfully the night before. Long after she'd arrived home and gone to bed, she'd lain there thinking of the past and the future she'd expected with Judd.

Impatient with this line of thinking, she flung the covers off and prepared to face the day. After dressing and making the bed, she ate a bowl of cereal, then carried her cup of coffee to the front porch to plan her day.

When the hardware store opened, she'd get a washer for the leaky faucet and fix that, she decided, settling into a wooden rocker with a cane bottom and back. She'd clean house, then go to the grocery store. Perhaps she'd go to the fairgrounds that afternoon and look over the livestock. She'd liked that as a kid. After that, Winona was supposed to come by and have pizza with her.

Satisfied that this was a workable plan that would keep her moderately busy, she finished the coffee while the sun pushed higher into the clear morning air. It was going to be a hot day.

She glanced at her shorts and knit top. They were okay for a trip to the hardware store. She took her cup into the house and turned off the coffeemaker. Removing the worn washer from the faucet, she slipped it into her pocket. She clipped her purse around her waist and decided to walk downtown rather than drive.

At the hardware store, she bought a packet of washers that matched the old one. As she was leaving, a man walked up to her.

"Hello, Tracy, remember me?"

She looked into a familiar face. Dark eyes. Dark hair, worn rather long. Jeans. A blue shirt open to the waist. "Wolf Boy," she said before she thought.

A wry grimace briefly twisted the mobile lips of the good-looking young man who'd greeted her. "Smile when you say that, partner," he said with mock menace.

She grinned. "Rafe, how are you?" Memories leap-frogged over each other into her mind.

Her father had interviewed the Rawlings clan out on Whispering Pines Road about their early life in Montana, so she was familiar with the family history. Rafe had been adopted.

Tracy had been around eight years old the summer an abandoned child had been found in the woods north of the Rawlings ranch. That child had been Rafe.

The newspapers and TV stations had made a field day of his discovery, calling him "Wolf Boy," a nickname that stuck, and writing the most incredible stories about him growing up with the wild animals. What drivel. He'd been a baby at the time. No clues to his real parentage had ever turned up.

"Long time no see," he said. "I'd heard you were in town."

"Temporarily," she said. "Are you ranching?"

"Not entirely. I'm a detective here in Whitehorn."

"I didn't know that."

"You and Lily Mae didn't get to the folks who live on the west side of the county when you had dinner the other night?" His smile was wry. He'd been a topic of speculation all his life and had become a quiet, reserved little boy; he seemed the same as a man.

"I don't think we got outside the city limits."

"So what's happening with the bones?"

"Not much. I'd like to find the rest of the skeleton."

"You going to run DNA tests?"

"I don't know. The FBI doesn't like having its resources used without good reason."

"Meaning the budget is tight, so watch what you spend?"

"You got it. The local police department must operate like the federal government."

"Yeah. Things are tough all over." He glanced at the package in her hand. "You going into the repair business?"

"Just a washer on a leaky faucet."

She smiled fondly at him, remembering him as a toddler who'd followed her around when she had visited the ranch with her father. She'd played with him while the grown-ups talked. Twenty-eight years ago. Heavens, how the time did fly.

They walked outside and said goodbye. She started down the street on foot.

"Are you walking?" he called to her.

"Yes."

"Hop in. I'll give you a ride. I wanted to ask you a couple of questions, if you have time."

She sensed an edginess in his stance. "Okay," she agreed. She climbed into the pickup. He slammed the door and got in on the driver's side. He cranked up the engine and drove off.

They talked about the changes in the neighborhood on the way. It wasn't until he pulled into her drive that she realized she hadn't told him where she lived.

"It's a small town," was his comment when she mentioned this fact. "Besides, it's my job as a cop to know everyone's business."

"Hmm, maybe Lily Mae missed her calling. Perhaps I should mention the police department the next time I see her."

Rafe held up both hands. "I give," he declared. "Lily Mae would have the office running a lonely hearts club before the year was out. She's always trying to match people up."

"Yeah? Who has she chosen for you?" She led the way into the house and toward the kitchen.

He gave a snort of derision. "I keep a low profile where women are concerned."

Tracy studied him. She sensed a loneliness that matched her own. "Why would you do that? You're darned good-looking. The gals in the county must be real miffed if you never look at them."

"I never said I didn't look." His smile wasn't reflected in his eyes. "Marriage doesn't seem to work out. It's hard enough when you know a person, but someone like me... Who knows what my background is? I may be the son of the Son of Sam."

"You're not a killer," she told him sternly. "There's no such thing as bad blood. You're what you make of yourself."

"Enough. My past, or lack of one, is ancient history. Tell me how you got into forensic investigation."

"Like father, like daughter, I suppose. I spent my youth collecting old stories with him. Ancient ways interested me more than modern times. I also liked working puzzles of any kind. Put those two together. Forensic investigation is sort of like working jigsaw puzzles. You just keep moving things around until you get all the pieces to fit."

"Someone said the bones from the res weren't old."

Tracy rolled her eyes, exasperated with the local grapevine. "Coffee?" she asked.

"Got any iced tea? The day is already hot."

She checked the refrigerator. The tea pitcher was nearly full. She poured two glasses.

"Were the bones old?" he asked.

"No. My guess is they've been in the ground twenty or thirty years. No more."

"How can you tell?"

"Stain penetration into the surface. Also I'd say the bones have been in a protected place. They're in too good a condition to have been out in the open all this time."

"Animals would have eaten them," he suggested.

"Right. There are some fresh teeth marks, but no real damage. The bones are too old to be tasty." She removed the packet of washers from her purse and laid them next to the sink.

"Here, let me change those washers for you," Rafe said. He put his glass on the counter and checked the leaky faucet. "May as well do both sides. Got a screwdriver?"

"I found a box of tools under the sink." She bent and got them out. "There's no need. I know how to fix it."

"The independent woman, huh?" He gave her an assessing glance. "Come on. Let me feel I have some use in the world."

She laughed while he made sure the water was off and unscrewed the cold-water handle. He quickly and efficiently replaced the washers in both faucets.

"There," he said upon finishing. "Just in the nick of time." He held up the other one to show her it was worn almost through the rubber and would have started leaking soon.

"What do I owe you for this great service?"

He gestured toward the cabinets while he stored the toolbox under the sink again. "How about two of those chocolate-chip cookies I saw in there when you got the glasses?"

"Hmm, you are observant. I'd better watch what I let you see in the future."

They chatted while she got out cookies. Rafe retrieved his glass and headed for the table. She did the same. Into this comfortable idle another presence intruded, in the form of the sheriff.

Judd came to the back door. His furious gaze met her startled one just as she turned from the counter. Iced tea slopped out onto the floor. "Judd!" she exclaimed.

Rafe went over and opened the door. "Come in, Sheriff."

"Thanks," Judd said laconically. He smiled coolly.

Tracy wondered if that momentary glimpse of anger had been in her imagination. "We're having cookies. Would you like to join us?" she asked, placing the glass on the table.

"No, thanks. I gave 'em up when I outgrew my morning nap."

"Uh-oh," Rafe said in a loud whisper to her. "Me thinks the boss is madder than hell."

She realized Judd was throwing out a challenge and the younger man wasn't backing down. She wasn't sure what to do.

Judd scowled, then turned a deadly eye on Tracy. "I came over earlier to fix the faucet. No one was home."

"I was at the hardware store," she explained, then frowned. She didn't have to account to him. Irritated with herself, she used more vigor than necessary to wipe up the spilt tea.

"The faucet is fixed," Rafe announced.

Tracy noticed his keen gaze studying Judd, as if he were judging his reaction to this news. She looked at the older lawman. He was in control. Other than the remnants of irritation at the wasted trip, no emotion showed on his lean, handsome face.

Judd glanced at the leftover coffee in the pot, then at her. "I'll take some coffee, if it isn't too much trouble."

"Not at all." She poured a cup, heated it in the microwave and handed it to him. When she went to the table again, Judd joined her, holding her chair for her before taking the one on her right.

"Moonlighting as a plumber?" Judd inquired of Rafe after watching the young officer down two cookies and reach for another.

Tracy drank her tea. Her appetite had fled.

"No. I was curious about the bones from the res. Tracy was telling me about forensics. See?" Rafe inquired innocently. "All in-the-line-of-duty stuff. Nothing clandestine going on."

Tracy was both amused and appalled at his effrontery. She saw Judd give Rafe a glance from under his eyebrows that had always boded ill for Thadd when the boy did something wrong. She tried to think what she could do to head off a collision between the men.

"The res isn't in your jurisdiction," Judd remarked.

"Yours either, Sheriff."

The two men locked eyes in silent combat.

"I need to go to the grocery store, then I thought I'd go out to the fair to look at the livestock," Tracy put in hurriedly. "Thanks for fixing the leak, Rafe. Remember me to your mom next time you see her." She stood, causing the men to rise, and urged the younger man toward the door.

Rafe grinned at her, then winked. "I'll see you at the fair. Shall I look for you by the calf pens, say...about one?"

"Yes," she said, practically pushing him out the door. *Men.*

He left. In a minute, she heard his pickup fire up and back out of the drive. The sound of its engine faded as he drove off. She turned toward the table with a frown.

"What was that all about?" she demanded.

"What? These cookies are good. Did you make them?"

"No. Why were you rude to Rafe?"

Judd stopped concentrating on the cookie he was dunking in his coffee and stuck the rest of it in his mouth. He gave her such a falsely innocent look that it disconcerted her.

"Me? Rude?"

Their son had assumed the exact same expression when he was trying to wiggle out of trouble. Like father...

"What?" he asked, his voice suddenly deeper as if he sensed the stab of pain the thought had caused her.

"I...nothing. Just a thought."

He studied her for a long minute. "How did Rafe happen to drop by and fix your sink?"

She explained that they'd met at the store. "I used to play with him when he was a baby. I'd entertain him while my father went through the Rawlings family albums. It was such a long time ago, and now...now he's a policeman. It's hard to believe."

"You didn't seem to be thinking of him as a baby when you made a date for the fair," Judd commented.

"I'm eight years older than he is." She gave Judd a puzzled glance. "I didn't make a date with him."

"I'm eight years older than you," Judd reminded her. "He said he'd meet you at the calf pens at one."

"Oh, that. He was just riling you." She tilted her head at a slight angle and studied her ex-husband. "Did he succeed?" she asked and wondered why she was deliberately trying to needle him.

"Hardly." Judd took a drink of coffee, seemingly as cool as a mountain breeze, all emotion now gone.

She watched his throat work as he swallowed. Once she'd loved to kiss him there, the faint taste of salt on her tongue when she'd nibbled and licked his freshly shaved skin. She looked away.

"Well, I have to make out a grocery list," she announced.

Judd made no effort to leave after her broad hint.

She set about the task, ignoring the man who watched her as she went through the cabinets and refrigerator for supplies. She didn't want to get too many staples. She'd have to toss them out when she left or haul them all the way back to California with her.

"Are you going to the fair this afternoon?" he asked after a lengthy silence.

"Yes, I think so."

"I have to drive down to Billings to check on some stolen items that have been recovered. I thought you might want to ride along. You used to like that."

She stared at him, trying to figure out why he'd asked her. She knew he was keeping an eye on her because of the case, but was that the only reason?

The old attraction was still there, as strong as ever...maybe stronger. That could have been jealousy she'd seen in Judd's eyes when he'd arrived and found Rafe at her kitchen table.

Surely not. Other than the lingering traces of a passion too strong to be forgotten, there was nothing between them.

A tremor of unease went through her. At thirty-six, she found she wasn't half as sure of life and love as she'd been at nineteen.

"Well?" he muttered in a growl.

She glanced around the kitchen. "I have too much to do. I still have to clean house...and—and go to the store...."

A tumult of emotions hit her, so fast, so hard, she couldn't figure out the individual ones. She stole a glance at Judd.

He sat like a statue at the table, the planes of his face rigid, his thoughts unreadable. She wanted to ask him what he was thinking, why he'd invited her on the trip, but she didn't.

She'd learned long ago that Judd didn't share his deepest feelings with her. Once she'd needed him desperately. Once she'd begged him to talk to her, to help her get past the grief that ravaged her soul. He'd walked out.

It had destroyed something in her, having him turn his back on her.... She fought back the tears that burned her eyes. That had been long ago. It didn't matter now. Their lives had separated into two diverging paths.

He nodded and stood. "Here. I brought you a timer. Set it to turn a lamp on around dusk." He laid it on the table.

She was aware of his gaze running over her, dark, sensual, almost brooding. It made her feel tight and achy inside, and so full of longing the tears rose again. "Thanks."

He walked out, taking his toolbox and packet of washers with him. She felt the increasing distance between them as an abyss of utter darkness, too wide to cross, as he got into his truck and left.

Judd cursed all the way to the office. Why the hell had he asked Tracy to come along with him? Insanity, pure insanity.

Or jealousy? a part of him asked.

He didn't want to think about it. He unlocked his office and collected the inventory of the item he was to pick up. He studied the list. Truthfully, the trip could wait until Monday. Or he could send a deputy.

Hearing laughter on the street, he paused and looked out the window at a couple who'd stopped to let their two kids play. He watched them for several minutes while the emptiness inside shifted uneasily.

It was getting harder to maintain that vacuum, he admitted. Being around Tracy punched holes in his self-control.

Passion. He still wanted her. It burned in him like a steady flame, refusing to go out. Passion was all right, but a man would be a fool to get mixed up in all that emotional baggage again.

All he'd felt was an echo of male possessiveness. Seeing Rafe hanging around Tracy had stirred primitive urges he'd do better to ignore. Tracy wasn't his. He didn't want her to be.

He sat at his desk and went over the current cases on his agenda. There'd been a couple of car thefts, some vandalism involving spray paint, a couple of domestic-violence calls. All those were solved or under investigation.

The bones from the reservation were the biggest question mark. Winona's vision had convinced him the case was homicide.

That led to the problem of Tracy. She was so damned independent. She didn't want him interfering with *her* case.

Too bad. He was going to keep her under his watchful eye whether she liked it or not. This was his county, his people. He was responsible for them. And for her as long as she was in the area.

Darkness seemed to open within him when he thought of her leaving again. He cursed under his breath. He'd ignore the tension between them and keep his mind strictly on the law.

Restless, he checked the time and headed out the door. He'd go talk to Winona. Now *there* was a woman with a man's mind—practical and sane, not running on temperament, but logic.

Yeah, he'd go talk to her. About the case.

She was concluding a deal when he parked next to the lopsided sign out front. She and the Cheyenne shook hands and laughed, then the man departed, giving a quick nod to Judd when he passed on the way to his pickup with a wheelbarrow full of junk.

"Business looks good," he commented as he surveyed the new items in the yard.

"It is," she agreed. "Look at this blanket."

Judd admired the Indian blanket she held up, which was woven with a Navajo design. The tourists wouldn't know the difference, or care if they did, he thought cynically. "Nice," he said.

"I'm going to enter it in the fair for his wife." She nodded toward the road as the pickup disappeared around a bend. "It'll fetch a fair price whether it wins a ribbon or not."

"Good."

"You're in a foul mood," Winona said. "Come have some chamomile tea with honey. It'll soothe your nerves."

Judd followed her across the crowded yard, keeping a sharp eye out for the goats. They liked to sneak up on him and butt him from behind, hitting him right in the back of the knee, which caused his leg to buckle. He'd bashed his kneecap on a concrete birdbath the last time that had happened.

Winona led the way inside the trailer. It always surprised him how neat and orderly it was compared to the front yard. The backyard was an oasis of flowers and peace.

They chatted about the weather and the fair while she fixed the tea. When she handed him the cup, her fingers brushed his. She jerked back as if burned.

He set the cup down and prepared to catch her, but she shook her head, telling him she was all right.

"You've been with Tracy," she said.

"Yeah. I saw her briefly this morning."

"Why are you angry with her?"

"I'm not—" He stopped abruptly when she cast a penetrating gaze on him, reminding him of a teacher he'd had in the fifth grade who could detect mischief before it got started. He swallowed. "She was with Rafe Rawlings."

Winona sat in her favorite chair and motioned for him to be seated. He chose a straight-backed chair at the table, pulling it around so he could face his hostess.

"You shouldn't have let her go," Winona said, quite gently for her. She usually was pretty blunt with him.

He felt the emptiness whirl and waited for it to settle. "I'm not here to talk about that. It's...those days are gone."

"But not forgotten," she said with some asperity, sounding more her usual self.

He shrugged, unwilling to discuss it. What good would it do? The past was long gone. There was no way to get it back at this late date. Not that he wanted to.

"You want to know about Tracy," Winona guessed correctly. "You want to know if she's in danger. The answer is yes."

His pulse leapt like a startled rabbit. "What? Who?"

She shook her head. "I don't know. I sensed it on her. Did she tell you of the first vision I had, the one from the other night when she came out for supper?"

"No." Judd felt a chill crept over him. His lethal streak, Sterling called it.

When he was on a case, a certain coolness would sometimes come over him. His mind would become as clear as crystal. He would be able to make connections between facts that few others seemed to notice. However, in this case it felt more like fear. Tracy in danger...

Winona related the vision of the two-faced woman.

"A lot of people are two-faced," he mused when she finished. "They pretend to be one thing when they're really another. Or they say one thing when they mean something entirely different."

Tracy had acted as if she loved him more than life itself, but when the chips were down, she'd turned from him without a backward glance. Not that he blamed her. He was the one who'd encouraged Thadd to be independent and unafraid.

When the doctor had walked out of the operating room and shaken his head wearily, telling them their child was gone, her love had died, too. Sometimes he thought he'd never gotten over those twin blows—the loss of his son and the loss of his wife.

A hand touched his.

He glanced into wise brown eyes and saw sympathy. A pressure built behind his eyes. Hurriedly, he took a drink of the hot tea.

"Things will work out," Winona said. Her gaze took on a misty quality. "I see darkness ahead. Tracy..." She paused, frowned, then shook her head.

"What did you see?" he asked, his heart slamming against his breastbone.

"Nothing. Just a feeling." She studied Judd as they sipped the soothing brew. "You're going to have to confront your sorrow someday," she advised.

The cup jerked, and hot tea sloshed over his hand. He grabbed a napkin and mopped it up. "What sorrow?" he asked, keeping his tone neutral. Too many emotions were being stirred up nowadays. He didn't need an old woman that half the county thought was batty telling him about his emotions.

"There's an emptiness in your soul," she murmured, partially closing her eyes. A cat jumped into her lap, and she stroked it absently. "It can be filled. But the filling will be painful, and the cost high."

The chill shot right down into his backbone. "I like the emptiness," he said in a low growl, feeling like a cornered wolf. "Life is easier that way."

"None of the pain?"

"That's right," he agreed harshly.

"But none of the joy," the wise woman reminded him gently. "Grab the joy while it's available. I let it go. In the end, I had only a month with the man I loved."

Judd looked at the old woman, startled. He'd never really thought of her being in love.

She smiled sadly. "Yes, even I was once in love. I'd never told another person until recently, and now I've told two."

"Tracy," he said, knowing at once who the other person had been. "There's something special between the two of you. Her mother commented on it once. She said she felt almost jealous of the bond you had with her daughter."

Winona merely nodded her head and rocked quietly back and forth, stroking the cat, whose purr filled the silence.

He sighed, then stood. "I'm going to Billings to pick up some stolen goods that have been recovered. Would you like to ride along?" He glanced around the neat trailer. "Or do you need to clean house, too?"

She laughed in delight at his irony. "So she turned you down. Don't be discouraged. Keep an eye on her. Twice I've sensed danger near her. Stay close."

"I will," he heard himself solemnly promise.

Later, driving back to Whitehorn from Billings, the crate of stolen guns in the back seat, he thought of his conversation with the psychic. God, he'd sounded as if he'd taken an oath to find the Holy Grail.

His feelings toward Tracy were the result of two things. One, since he was sheriff of the county, naturally he felt protective toward her. Two, there was a lingering passion between them.

Well, hell, nice to know some things in life never changed. Although desire wasn't one of the things he'd have voted for, given a choice.

After leaving the stolen loot with the officer in charge of the evidence storage room in the basement of the police station, he headed for the fairgrounds five miles south of town.

He found Tracy at the calf pens, laughing while she tried to pet a calf that was trying to suck her fingers. Rafe Rawlings stood beside her, one hand at her waist as she bent over the low fence.

White heat shot through Judd, followed by a coldness that left his mind crystal clear. He walked forward.

* * *

Tracy straightened up and glanced around, feeling suddenly uneasy. Her eyes met a dark and dangerous gaze.

"Hello, Judd," she said, her voice fairly steady.

"'Lo, the lawman returneth," Rafe drawled, earning him a sardonic smile from the sheriff.

"In the flesh," Judd returned with cool nonchalance.

Tracy gave each man a warning frown. She was not going to be a bone fought over by two dogs…or cops, in this case. She didn't understand why men had to be so territorial in the first place.

She had decided that was the root of the earlier jealousy—if it had been jealousy she'd seen in Judd at her house. Anyway, she was going to choose her own companions.

Rafe had been asking her a million questions about forensic techniques and about the bones she was examining. She'd promised to let him see them and to explain some of the things she looked for when she was doing an investigation. As a local policeman, he was naturally curious about murder in his backyard, so to speak.

Judd, of course, thought the case should be his. It galled him that the reservation was in the county, but out of his jurisdiction. Tough. He would have to accept her authority just as the tribal council had had to.

"I'd like to see the rabbits now. The ribbons were supposed to be posted on them by noon," she said brightly.

The two men fell into step with her. They admired the rabbits, the pigeons, chickens, turkeys and ducks. She wandered over to the ring, where prize breeding stock was being judged.

She noticed Judd checking the security at the fair. Several deputies were in evidence. Their presence would do a lot toward ensuring a peaceful gathering. She saw him nod to each lawman they met. Most of them returned his greeting with a casual salute.

The two men were still with her when she spied Winona in the bleachers watching the judging. "Hello. I didn't expect to see you until tonight," she said, sitting by the older woman.

Rafe slid onto the bench beside her before Judd got a chance to. Judd's lips tightened fractionally, then he sat down in front of Tracy on the next bench and twisted around to talk to the other three.

"I got the honey collected, put in jars and labeled, so I decided to come in. I entered a pie in the fall-fruit-baking category—pumpkin and honey with wild nuts."

"My favorite," Judd muttered. "And you didn't even offer me a piece when I was out there."

"I didn't make it until later. Besides, I couldn't take a piece out of it and then put it in the contest." She gave him a grin that drew crinkles around her eyes in a merry fashion. She looked like an elf with her sun-browned face and plump figure.

"I wonder if the judges will leave any after they taste it," he grumbled.

"Leftovers go to the senior-citizen centers," Rafe put in.

"I made one to give to Tracy," Winona said with an innocent smile. "Maybe, if you're real nice, she'll give you some of it."

Judd glanced at Tracy. She saw him hesitate. "I'll buy that pizza you promised Winona for supper," he declared, "if you'll serve the pie for dessert."

"All right," she agreed.

"Great," Rafe said, counting himself in. "I'll get the ice cream to go on the pie."

Tracy choked back laughter at the look Judd gave the young policeman. Winona had no such compulsions. She cackled aloud.

After a second, Judd grinned and dodged a mock punch from Rafe, who was also laughing.

Sterling and Jessica McCallum joined them and demanded to know what the joke was.

"Two dogs and one bone," Winona told them.

Jessica glanced at the two men, then at Tracy. She grinned in delight and plopped down by Judd. "Looks like an even number of dogs and bones to me," she announced, clearly putting the men in the dog category.

Her husband groaned and demanded to know how much of this stuff a man was supposed to take. That earned him a poke in the side from his wife.

The day ended with all of them going to the pizza place for dinner, then trooping back to Tracy's cottage for pie and ice cream. Jennifer played with several plastic bowls and a wooden spoon that Tracy gave her. After eating some ice cream, she went to sleep on the sofa.

The adults took their coffee out on the porch afterward and watched the sky darken from twilight into night. Rafe managed to stay at her side most of the time, which paired Judd with Winona.

Tracy felt a rush of pride as he escorted the older woman, who had to be in her late seventies, with all the gallantry of a knight of old guarding a princess.

After everyone left, she put the dishes in the dishwasher, then changed into her sleep set of satin tap pants and matching green top. She fastened a floral robe over it.

A knock at the back door startled her.

"Judd," she murmured, seeing his stern face beyond the small glass panes across the top of the door. She unlocked the dead bolt and let him in. "I didn't hear your truck. Did you forget something?"

"No." He thrust his hands into his pockets. "I walked over. There was something I wanted to talk to you about."

"Yes?"

"Why the hell didn't you tell me Winona sensed you were in danger?"

She stared at him in total surprise. "It wasn't a definite thing," she finally explained. "I mean, it was probably vibes she was getting from the bones."

Judd shook his head. "It's you. I talked to her earlier today. She said *you* were in danger."

"Did she see something?" While Tracy heeded the wise woman's visions, she wasn't sure about feelings. They could be deceptive. Once she'd thought Judd loved her more than anything, but since that time, she'd learned to distrust turbulent emotions.

"No," he admitted.

"Well, then . . ."

She stood in the middle of the kitchen floor, not sure what to say. Nervous flutters chased through her stomach at his silent stance. She tightened the tasseled belt of the robe.

He took a step toward her. His hands clenched and unclenched at his sides while his eyes devoured her.

She felt his gaze move over her, burning into every inch. A hot tide of longing ran through her. She might not trust her feelings, but she couldn't deny them. She still wanted him with all the wild yearning of long ago.

He must have seen it in her eyes. "Trace," he murmured.

For once he looked as uncertain as she felt. He took another step toward her. She witnessed his struggle with the force that had drawn them together from the first moment they'd met.

Bewilderment joined the other emotions that roiled in her. She didn't understand it—this irresistible magic that leapt into being whenever they met. She didn't want it.

She fought it and knew he was doing the same.

"No," she whispered, dredging up every ounce of willpower. "It's not...we can't."

The planes of his face abruptly seemed harsher, the bones pressing against his skin as if demanding to escape. "I know," he said with a bitter sigh. "Oh, God, I know."

He pivoted and crossed to the door in two long strides. She clutched the lapels of her robe, stifling the cry that rose in her, ignoring the part that wanted to ask him to stay.

He faced her, all iron control now. The tough sheriff in a tough situation. "You might be in charge of the case, but I'm still sheriff of this county. If your life is in danger, I'm going to do my damnedest to see that you aren't hurt...no matter what."

He went out, then stood on the other side of the door. When she didn't move, he rattled the knob impatiently. She rushed forward and locked the door. He nodded, then headed off into the dark, cutting through the woods in the moonlight.

Tracy turned out the inside lights, made sure the porch lights were on, then went to bed. She lay there a long time, worrying about the situation.

The pressure was building between them. When it got too great, what would happen?

Anxiety swept over her. She wanted to leave. She wanted to solve the case and get out of there...before it was too late.

Six

The Sunday paper arrived with a thud on the front porch. Tracy pushed her hair back and peered at the clock. Barely past seven. She groaned, tossed the covers off and headed for the bathroom. A shower would wake her up.

Later, after eating a breakfast of cereal and banana, she read the news from beginning to end. She folded the paper and stacked it neatly in the middle of the table.

She sighed. The sound seemed to echo through the empty house. Honestly, she never thought she'd see the day she missed the friendly *drip-drip* of a faucet!

Shoving back the chair, she stood and walked out on the front porch. It was almost ten. Down the street, she saw a family come out of their house and get in their car. The parents and two little girls were dressed in their Sunday clothes. Probably on their way to Sunday school, she thought.

She watched them until the car disappeared down the lane. They'd looked so happy. With a soft gasp, she realized she was envious of their good fortune.

Stepping off the porch, she strolled around the yard, admiring the roses and daisies. Finally, the silence was more than she could take. She paused in her restless pacing and looked down the lane toward the south.

There was a place she'd been avoiding. She knew she'd have to go there before she left town. The psychologist had told her she had to face the past in order to get on with her life.

All right, she resolved, gathering her courage. She would.

Going inside, she clipped on her purse, rubbed sunscreen into her face and arms, donned a hat and started out.

She walked south along Pale Bluff Lane until she came to Willow Brook Road. She crossed the road and headed west until she reached a small chapel, which faced the street. The Whitehorn cemetery surrounded the natural-stone building.

Stopping, Tracy clasped the wrought-iron fence that surrounded the rolling acres and let her gaze roam from the stained-glass windows of the chapel to the delicate carving of twin angels set on the support columns at the entrance gate.

Past the entrance, benches were placed under shade trees in the cultivated lawn, and row after row of headstones marched over the rolling meadow.

Her hands trembled, but she opened the gate and went in. She walked down the path paved with river gravel, the sound of her steps carried away on the warm sigh of the breeze.

At last, in the newer section, she came to a site marked with four polished-granite columns at the corners. Inside the area, a small rectangle was squared off with granite posts set almost flush to the ground.

She sat on one of the taller columns and stared off at the mountains to the west. Part of a Bible verse she'd learned as a child came to her. *I will lift up mine eyes unto the hills.*

Sometimes the sight of mountains and far vistas offered comfort to her soul, but not today.

She swallowed hard, then looked at the low granite stone set at the head of the small rectangle and read the inscription.

Thaddeus Roper Hensley. Beloved Son.

The breeze sighed through the trees, and for a second she thought she heard his laughter, radiant with the delight he'd found in life, in the shear joy of living. She listened intently.

The crunch of gravel was the only sound that came to her. She pivoted on the narrow seat.

Judd stood on the path. He held a pot of golden-eyed daisies in his hand. He walked forward slowly as if he thought she might bolt if he came too close.

"I sometimes plant flowers," he said.

Her throat closed. She nodded and watched as he pulled a trowel from the back pocket of his jeans and planted a bright clump of flowers at each side of the headstone.

When he finished, he sat cross-legged on the grass near her feet and pulled a few tiny weeds from the grave.

"I wondered if you'd come." He looked at her then.

She saw the darkness in the depths of his eyes and knew it came from the soul. She lifted a hand, instinctively needing to soothe the pain with a caress. She let it fall back into her lap.

"I had to." She breathed deeply, carefully, holding on to a control that seemed intent on slipping if she didn't watch it. The need to weep rose in her until it became an ache.

He nodded.

"I still miss him," she heard herself confess, although she hadn't meant to mention it at all. "His laughter. His curiosity and endless questions. His love of all living things. I miss him. It's like...a cold and lonely place inside."

The tendons stood out in Judd's neck. She knew he didn't like to talk about it, but she couldn't seem to stop. The words, like the tears, pressed forward.

"I miss him, and . . . I'm angry with him." She clenched her hands together. "I'm angry with him for going off into the woods. He knew he wasn't allowed to go off like that by himself. I want him to come home with that sheepish look he got when he knew he was in trouble. I want to send him to bed without his supper. I want to ground him for a month—"

Judd stood abruptly, his fists clenched at his sides, his face as tight-looking as it had been the day before.

She stood, too.

He looked at her so long she began to feel they would turn to stone and stand there forever, locked together in mutual despair, yet apart, always apart.

"Trace," he said hoarsely. He made a movement with his hand, as if he wanted to reach for her, then dropped it.

The gulf of time and unshared grief stretched between them. A quiver of need fell into the darkness inside her like a stone into an abyss. She longed for warmth, for light in her soul.

Once she'd needed him, but he'd walked away. If he walked away now, she'd never forgive him. . . .

No, she had no right to think that. Everything was over between them. They were strangers now, although they'd once created a child together.

She stared at the distant hills and swallowed against the ache inside. "I miss him," she whispered. "Our little boy. I miss him." She fought the darkness, but it closed over her.

* * *

Judd felt the blackness rise from the pit inside him. He'd thought the emptiness was safe, but that had been a delusion. He knew that now. The pain had been there all along, waiting for a chance to escape and consume him again.

He wanted to leave, to walk away and not have to think about the past. But he couldn't. Not this time. He was going to have to face her grief, and perhaps, in facing hers, he'd have to face his, too. The cold and lonely place she spoke of he knew lay at the bottom of the pit. It was where the pain dwelt.

Once, she'd asked him to tell her how to stop hurting, and he'd had no answer. He still didn't.

Not knowing how to comfort her, he'd left her to deal with the terrible grief on her own. Perhaps that had been the end of their marriage, not later, when she'd turned from his touch in loathing, as he'd thought. This time, he knew he couldn't leave.

She put her hands over her face. He realized she was weeping, although she made no sound. He lifted a hand, let it drop. He felt helpless in the face of her anguish.

"Trace," he said, searching for the words he hadn't been able to find in the past. "Don't. Crying...it doesn't do any good. It doesn't change things."

But she was beyond hearing him. Her hat blew off, and her hair gleamed like new pennies in the noonday sun, reminding him of the young girl he'd fallen instantly in love with.

She still didn't make a sound, but stood there with her hands covering her face, as if to hide the grief...from him, he realized. She didn't want him to see her cry.

He knew he couldn't walk away this time. He had to face the pain. He had to face it and deal with it . . . or damn her to the same emptiness he felt inside. She deserved more of life than that.

Swallowing hard, he stepped close to her. He touched her hair and gently stroked it, then down her back. She didn't jerk away.

He felt the tremors that ran through her slender body like shock waves through metal. He'd never seen her cry, not like this, as if her heart were dying inside her.

He felt a moment of panic as his own control slipped. The pressure that had been building inside rushed over him. He pressed his fingers to the bridge of his nose, trying to fight the weakness of tears. Tears . . . what good did they do?

And yet he knew they were needed . . . that Tracy needed them. . . . He had to help her, to save her from the dark hell that lived in his own soul. . . .

God help him, he thought, and didn't know if it was a prayer for her or for himself.

He took her into his arms, cradling her grief against his body, trying to absorb it, to control it with his will. When she wrapped her arms around him and pressed her face against his neck, laving him with her own tears, he was lost.

"Trace, oh, God, Trace," he whispered, while blackness devoured him from the inside out.

Her arms tightened around him. He felt her warmth, the tremors that racked her slender body. The pressure built inside until he could no longer control it. He pressed his face into her hair and held her as closely as he could.

When the storm was over, she leaned into him as if exhausted by the silent weeping. For a while, she rested in his arms, and for those moments, a strange sense of peace washed over him.

"I miss him," she said again, quieter this time. It sounded like a final goodbye.

He had to clear his throat to speak. "I know."

She leaned back against his arms and looked at him. Her lashes outlined her eyes in wet spikes as she gazed up at him. He saw the trembling of her fingers as she reached up.

He held very still.

With the gentlest of touches, she traced the wetness on his lower lashes. He returned her gaze without looking away.

"You miss him, too," she said, rubbing the moisture between her fingers until it was gone.

"Yes." To his own ears his voice seemed far off, a distant rumble in his chest. He cleared his throat.

"Sometimes I wondered."

He dropped his arms and stepped back, too stunned to speak.

"You never..." She spread her hands in a helpless gesture. "You were always so... silent, so controlled."

The wind shifted, and patterns of dappled light danced over them. He studied the patterns, looking for answers to the silent questions between them.

The emptiness swirled uneasily inside him. It was no longer a haven from pain and hadn't been since her return. He realized the peace he thought he'd found had been but an illusion.

As for the control she spoke of, he'd lost that when she'd covered her face and wept. Even thinking about her pain caused a tightening in his chest.

She dropped to her knees and plucked at some weeds among the grass blades. When she ran her fingers over the grass, he was reminded of how she'd once run her fingers through Thadd's hair to smooth it into place. She'd loved their son... and so had he.

He tried to find words to tell her how he'd felt. It was so damned hard to say it out loud.

"You didn't give me credit for loving him," he finally said, remembering that last desperate year together and some of the hurtful things they'd said.

She sat back on her heels and looked up at him. The sun lighted her hair into a glowing nimbus. Her eyes gleamed like green agates in her pale face. "What do you mean?"

"You seemed to think only a mother could hurt, that only a mother could miss her child until each day took more effort than it was worth to continue living." He paused and drew a deep, careful breath. "A father could never miss a child that much, hurt like that. Isn't that what you thought?"

"I never...Judd, I never thought that." She lifted her hand as if she wanted to touch him, but she didn't.

"You never forgave me." He gave a bitter snort and forced the words from a tight throat. "I can't say that I blame you. I never forgave myself."

She did touch him then. Rising, she caught his face between her hands and made him look at her. "I never blamed you." She said each word clearly and firmly. "Never."

"I was the one who laughed at your fears," he reminded her, bringing it all out in the open. "I was the one who took him hunting and let him roam the woods."

For an eternity, he stared into her eyes. She held his gaze, letting him look into her soul. He saw the truth in her. Or maybe he needed it so badly he thought he saw her forgiveness.

"Never," she repeated.

A light clicked on inside him, a dim one—the tiny flickering of a firefly seen through a storm—but it was there.

He had needed to hear her say it. He'd needed her to forgive him....

It was a startling thought. He drew back from it. He'd made a life for himself that was bearable. He didn't need anything more. It was Tracy who'd needed comforting, not the other way around. Perhaps now that she'd faced this moment, she could get on with her life and find a future of happiness.

For a second, hope flared in him. He tamped it down. Not him. He wanted it for Tracy, not himself. His life was okay like it was. Not exciting, but . . . safe.

That is, it would be when she left again.

He turned his head, and she let him go. He looked at the mountains until the mist cleared from his eyes.

"I think I'll go now. I had to come." She paused. "I wonder if we would have made it, all those years ago, if we'd cried in each other's arms then."

Leaving him with this thought, she started along the path. He watched her, then knew he couldn't let her leave, not just yet. There was something else he had to say.

He picked up the trowel and empty flower pots, then spotted her hat. He retrieved it and hurried to catch up with her.

At the chapel, he opened the gate, then closed it behind him. He saw her perusal of the sports car at the curb. "It's nearly time for lunch," he said. "There's this place I know that serves the best fried shrimp in the state. You interested?"

One hand went to her face as if checking for damages. Her eyes were a little red and her nose was pink, but she still looked beautiful. She glanced at her clothes. He could see the refusal forming before she spoke.

"You look fine," he told her, feeling stubborn about her joining him for some reason.

"If you're sure," she said hesitantly.

"We can stop by the house so you can freshen up," he offered.

"Your house?" The idea clearly startled her.

"I meant the cottage."

"Oh." She nodded.

He unlocked the car, and they climbed in. At the house, he waited outside while she went in. In less than five minutes, she was back. He'd always liked that in her. She never kept a man waiting for hours while she preened in front of a mirror.

Driving along the highway, soft music on the radio, he went over what he wanted to say to her, but it wasn't until they were far up in the mountains that he spoke.

"There was a time when you wanted to talk to me, but I walked out. I've wanted to tell you I'm sorry for that for a long time." He swallowed as the words balled in his throat. "It was just...I couldn't talk then, not about Thadd."

She didn't answer for a long time. "I understand," she said at last in a voice that told him she did.

Another load seemed to dissolve inside him. Funny, he hadn't realized he was carrying around such a heavy conscience. A sigh of relief escaped him.

"I knew you loved Thadd," she continued. "It showed in a hundred ways each and every day. I knew you had strong feelings. It was just that you never shared them with me. I needed...well, it doesn't matter now. We simply weren't at the same place at the same time, were we?" she mused aloud.

He suddenly wished they could go back to that day in the woods and start their lives over from that first meeting....

* * *

Tracy examined the slope of the bluff from the site where she'd found the new bones the previous week. If any bones had been buried farther up the slope and recently dug up and dragged down here by an animal, why didn't she see any signs of it?

Why take the bones to another place after digging them up?

Unless a bigger animal was in the vicinity and tried to take it, then the smaller one would head for cover with his prize.

She stretched her weary back. She'd spent most of the morning bent over, studying the ground for a clue. Bones didn't just appear from nowhere, unattached to the rest of the skeleton, without cause.

If she were to consider erosion, then she'd have to look further for signs of it. She started hiking up the hill.

A half hour later she emerged from the trees onto a grand escarpment of limestone that looked like the small end of a huge egg protruding from the ground. The limestone had cracked and buckled in several places, particularly along the tree line on the lower side of the slope.

She climbed to the top of the egg and sat down. From there she commanded a magnificent view of the surrounding territory—the reservation on the north, the Kincaid place to the south, the mountains sweeping westward and northward, and finally, the ribbon of highway that led back to town.

The air seemed cooler up here. When the sun dipped behind a cloud, she decided to eat her lunch.

Swinging her fanny pack around to the front, she removed an energy bar and a banana. While she ate, she thought of her lunch with Judd on Sunday. Three days ago. She hadn't seen him on Monday when she and

Winona watched the Fourth of July fireworks at the fair, but he'd been at the office yesterday and today.

Something had changed between them, she thought. She chewed a bite of energy bar and pondered the situation.

Like the rain, the tears they'd shed had cleared the air between them. Old questions had been answered or at least laid to rest. By the time he dropped her by the cottage that afternoon, they had been almost easy with each other.

Except for that smoldering hunger that wouldn't go away no matter how hard they tried to ignore it.

She swallowed, then sighed heavily. That hadn't changed, but he had managed to crack a joke about it when a couple had put some money in an old-fashioned jukebox and started dancing.

"If we danced to that, I'd have to arrest myself for indecent exposure," he'd murmured, listening to the theme from a movie they'd once seen together.

His disgruntled expression, as well as the complaint, had surprised her into laughing. Then he'd looked surprised that she'd found it amusing and had laughed, too.

"Such is life," she'd taunted.

So it is, she thought, sobering as she replayed the day in her mind. She'd done that often in the past seventy-two hours. There had been something sweet and poignant between them on the drive back to town.

At the cottage, she hadn't invited him in. Instead, he'd walked her to the door, handed her the hat she'd worn earlier, tipped his head and left.

But not before their eyes had met in a glance of mutual awareness. If he stayed much longer, they would end up making love. It was inevitable, like the ebb and flow of the tides. The forces of nature couldn't be stopped by the mere efforts of humans.

The worst part was she wasn't sure she wanted to stop it.

She sighed again and ate the banana and drank a small can of juice. She tucked the debris in a plastic bag and stuck it in the pack. Standing, she twirled the pack to her backside to keep it out of the way and started back to work.

Working around the limestone escarpment, she examined each nook and cranny of it, working in a spiral from the egglike top. Nothing in the cracks indicated a deeper opening underneath.

Slowly she moved lower, coming to the trees at the bottom edge where she'd first ascended. It looked like the accumulation of dirt and leaves had been recently disturbed. There were signs of erosion due to runoff from the limestone.

Finding a stick, she picked it up and poked at the buildup of leaves along an overhang. To her surprise, the stick went down a good ways.

After pulling her blue shirt off, she laid it and the pack aside, then started work in earnest. Little tingles of excitement went off inside her. She'd felt them before... when she was about to make a find.

She worked with a trowel and rock pick, carefully loosening the debris, then scraping it away. Sometimes it was hard not to rush right in, but she didn't want to damage any pieces.

Finally, she hit pay dirt... or rather, bone.

A femur, the long bone of a thigh. Now if she could just find the pelvis, she'd know for sure whether it was male or female and the approximate age.

She examined the femur before placing it beside her shirt and pack. From its thickness and length, it probably belonged to someone about five-ten to six feet. As she'd suspected from the thickness of the wrist bones, the skeleton was most likely that of a male.

DNA tests could tell her for sure, but so could the pelvis. She worked swiftly, removing the debris and placing it aside, making sure she wasn't overlooking any pieces. An hour passed.

She wiped the sweat off her forehead and took a break. It was while she was resting that she heard a "Hello-o-o" from below.

"Up here," she shouted.

A man came up through the woods. She recognized the broad shoulders and braids tied with leather strips before he emerged from the shadows under the trees a few yards away from her.

"Jackson, hello," she called to let him know where she was.

He spotted her and came over. "You've found something?" he asked, a tone of excitement underscoring the statement as he viewed her work under the ledge.

"Yes, a femur." She retrieved it and held it so he could visually examine it.

"Can you tell anything from it?"

"Um, yes." She became preoccupied with taking a closer look at the thick thigh bone. "I think it was a man, or a very tall, robust female. Young. There's no sign of deterioration in the joint. He was most likely a cowboy, or somebody used to sitting astride."

"Wow," Jackson said. "Anything else?"

She got out a bag from her pack and wrapped the bone, then turned back to the dig. "Not yet, but I'm hoping. The body was apparently concealed under this ledge...." She considered for a moment, then added, "Or he might have crawled in there for protection."

"Maybe he fell from his horse," Jackson suggested.

"And it was storming—"

"The wolves were after him—"

"Right. His leg was broken—"

"Could you tell that from the thigh bone? It looked okay to me."

She laughed. "No. I was just getting into the scenario." Sitting on the ground, she went back to work.

He dropped down on his haunches and peered under the shallow ledge. "Uncle Frank said to thank you for the reports you sent to the office. He was disappointed the bones weren't ancestors and said to tell you that you had permission to do any tests necessary to identify them, including DNA matching. He asked me to phrase this delicately, so here goes—could you have made a mistake about the age of the bones?" he asked bluntly, then grinned.

"You always did have a way with words," she remarked dryly. "There's no mistake. The bones aren't fossilized, not even on the surface. They're not old. You knew that."

"Yeah, but as an official of the tribe, I had to ask. Now that that's out of the way, do you want to come to the house Friday night? Maggie and I are having a cookout."

She was curious about Jackson's new wife. "I'd love to... if you promise me fry bread with honey."

"Pick up some honey from Winona and you're on. I'll do the fry bread myself."

"Your wife isn't Cheyenne?" That surprised her, considering that Jackson had once been married to a white.

"She's a city Injun," he explained. "She doesn't know fry bread from buffalo chips." He shook his head, as if wondering why he'd ever married such an ignorant woman.

Tracy saw the warmth in his eyes when he spoke of his wife and suppressed a jab of envy. "I'm looking forward to meeting her. Now, enough socializing. My boss will fuss if he finds me talking instead of digging."

"I'll help. Tell me what to do."

She glanced at his clothes. He wore old jeans and scuffed boots. His shirt had seen many washings. "Okay. Block off a square and take off one even layer at a time."

They worked companionably for an hour. She was reminded of her childhood days on the reservation. Jackson had been her best friend. They'd both loved it there and wanted to stay, but both of them had had to leave.

Strange, the turns life could take. He'd left and married, apparently never to return, while she'd married and moved close by. Then he'd divorced and returned, apparently to stay. She'd divorced and left, meaning never to come back.

Longing washed over her in a sudden deluge. She gripped her trowel and concentrated on digging until the emotion subsided.

"Hey," Jackson said. "Look."

She blinked away the memories and glanced over at his find. "The ilium! Don't move it!" she ordered when he tried to lift it.

He moved aside when she crowded in. Carefully, she dug out the debris around the bone. She lifted it out of the hole.

"It's complete," she murmured in satisfaction. She turned it, looking at it from every angle. "Yes...yes," she said, picking out clues as she examined the pelvic bone.

"Well?" Jackson demanded.

"Male. Less than twenty-five years old."

"Indian?"

She shrugged. "I don't know. Show me your thigh bone, and I'll make a comparison."

"Ha-ha," he said.

"Let's find the skull. It's bound to be here. With it, we can surely figure out who the cowboy was."

"I'll start a check of all the tribal missing-person reports," Jackson told her.

"Good. Now let's see what else we can find."

It was nearly dark before they gave up.

"Damn," Jackson said.

"My feelings, too." Tracy frowned at the hole.

They'd hit rock bottom. There was nothing else. She studied the area. He looked at his watch.

"Erosion," she muttered. "Look at the runoff patterns. This area under the ledge has eroded away where the water gushed through that crack." She pointed out the signs.

The shallow gully disappeared over the edge of the bluff. She and Jackson walked over and peered fifty feet down into the creek that meandered along the cliff base.

"So that's the end of it."

"Heck, no. Now I'll search the creek," she said.

"We'd better leave. It's getting late."

"Right." She packed up and headed for her car, the bones wrapped in special paper bags, then in plastic.

Like a kid with a treasure she wanted to show, she was eager to get to town. She said goodbye to Jackson and drove down the steep trail. She had to see Judd right away.

Seven

Judd looked at the clock, then at the darkening sky. Where the hell was Tracy? She was usually back from her digging around on the res well before dark.

Not that she had to report in to him...as she'd made damned clear more than once.

Hell, she'd probably gone to the tribal chairman's house for dinner. Frank Many Horses seemed to think of her as a long-lost daughter. Jackson Hawk thought a lot of her, too. Of course, Jackson had recently married, so he wasn't a rival—

Judd broke off the thought and cursed aloud as he realized what he was thinking. He closed his eyes and leaned back in the comfortable executive chair, his heels on the desk, and idly rocked to and fro while he tried to get his head straight.

There was nothing wrong with him that a little sleep wouldn't cure. *Or a long, satisfying tumble in the hay,* an insidious voice from some unbidden recess of his mind suggested.

Yeah, he admitted, that, too.

His dreams were a mixture of the old and the new—the old being the days and nights with Tracy when he'd been free to make love to her whenever he wished; the new being the days her perfume, her laughter, her womanly aura lingered in his office long after she took off for the res.

A hard pang whipped through him as his body reminded him all too forcibly that he was a man. The problem was Tracy. She was the one he wanted.

She'd been the most wonderful lover he'd ever had.

Not that there had been all that many. He was a naturally monogamous person. Maybe it was the way he'd been raised, or maybe it was something he'd learned from observing others, but he'd always felt that when two people were intimate enough to possibly produce a child, they owed respect to each other and that creative process.

He pressed his thumb and finger against his eyes, momentarily shutting out the headache that had plagued him all day, then looked at the clock again.

Where the hell was she?

Pivoting in the chair, he sat so he could see the street. Most of the parking spaces were empty. The stores didn't stay open past five o'clock on a weekday night. Farther along, there were two pickups and three cars in front of the local saloon.

He gave a snort of wry laughter. Sterling would have said he was being "bitchy." Maybe so, but, well, he was worried.

The courthouse clock chimed the hour. Seven. Maybe her car had broken down. Probably a flat tire. Or she'd run out of gas.

Tracy tended to live in her own world and forget the basics, things like eating, putting gas in the car and so forth. It hadn't bothered him while they were married.

She'd pleased him in so many other ways, he admitted. When he came home, she was always delighted to see him. The way she'd look up, her eyes wide and shining, as if he were Prince Charming in person . . . God, what it did to a man to be wanted like that.

He gritted his teeth and tried to close out the troublesome thoughts. He couldn't.

The memory of their lovemaking filled his nights. She'd been so responsive, loving everything he did...so natural.

Images flashed into his mind. Her hair flowing around her shoulders as she turned the tables on him. Her teasing smile as she made him lie still and let her have her way with him. The little crooning cries she'd made. The low murmurs of delight, telling him what she liked.

Yes, like that...no, slower...lower...there...oh, yes...oh, love, love...

He leapt to his feet, his body as rigid as a steel beam. It was no good thinking of what had been. It was over. Over.

The ringing of the telephone halted him in his tracks as he headed for the door. He grabbed the instrument, nearly yanking the cord out in his rush to answer.

"Hensley," he said.

"Judd?"

He took a calming breath. "Winona. What can I do for you?"

"Is Tracy there with you?" she asked.

The hairs stood up on the back of his neck. He forced himself to be calm. Nothing had happened to her. He'd know it if she were in trouble. He didn't pause to figure out this last cryptic thought.

"No. Do you want me to take a message for her?"

There was silence at the other end of the line. "She wasn't home when I tried her house," Winona told him, worry in her tone.

"What's wrong? Have you seen something?"

"It's more a feeling. I can't describe it. I just sense...I don't know. Danger, I think. It came to me a couple of hours ago. Did she find more bones? That seems to trigger it.''

"She's supposed to be at the reservation. Maybe I'll run out and check on her.''

"Would you?'' Winona requested. "I'd feel much better if I knew she was all right.''

"Sure. She's probably had car trouble. I'll check it out.''

They said goodbye. He locked his office and headed out the door. At the front steps, he stopped. A compact car, its metallic blue surface taking on a purple hue in the twilight, pulled to a stop across the street. Tracy hopped out.

He watched as she removed a package from the seat as if it were fragile and headed across, quickly glancing both ways. She saw him at the top of the steps and quickened her pace, a smile blooming on her expressive lips.

His heart rate speeded up, too.

There were dirt stains on the knees of her jeans and at her temple where she'd obviously pushed a wisp of hair out of her eyes. Her lipstick was gone, and her nose was pink from the sun. She was indescribably beautiful.

"Judd, wait till you see what Jackson found,'' she called out, holding her package out a little.

He waited for her, then fell into step with her as she headed for the building. "Jackson?''

"Um-hmm. He came by and helped me dig this afternoon.''

Judd had to unlock the outside door to let them in. They went through the silent corridor and up the steps to his office. He opened the door. She went through to the conference room, where she set her package on the table. "Look at this.''

She removed the two packages from the plastic bag, then laid her finds on the table. She smiled at him, her eyes wide and shining, filled with delight.

He bent over to hide the sudden sting of moisture in his eyes. Damn, but he'd have to get a grip on himself. The past was gone, and she wasn't in his future.

Her find was a femur and the pelvic saddle. He studied them for a couple of minutes. "Male?" he asked, venturing a guess.

He'd read a book on forensic anthropology once, not because her father had said she was studying it, he hastened to assure himself, but because it sounded like a subject a lawman ought to know a little about.

"Definitely. Early twenties."

"How can you tell?"

She picked up the pelvic bone. "See this Y-shaped junction here? The three main growth centers don't come together until the male is around twenty-five. The epiphyses are almost together but not quite. See?"

He studied the section she pointed out. Her hair brushed against his cheek as he bent closer. He ignored the tingles that radiated from the spot. Concentrating fiercely on the pelvis, he peered at the Y-shaped line she'd mentioned.

"Can you give me a more definite age?" he asked, trying not to notice the tantalizing scent of her. She smelled of earth and sunshine, of mountain air and pine resin...of sweat and musk and perfume...of *woman*.

"Yes. He was twenty-four years, three months, two days and eighteen minutes old when he died. Would you like the seconds, too?" She replaced the pelvis on the table.

He inhaled the essence of her deep into his lungs. It was like filling himself with life. He realized she was staring at him, her eyes changing as she noticed his absorption with her rather than the conversation.

Heat seeped into his neck as he tried to remember what she'd just said. Her words finally registered in his brain.

"Very funny." He tried to sound amused. He pushed his hands into his pockets and walked away.

"He was closer to twenty-five than twenty," she told him in a softer tone.

"I see."

"I'm going to ask for another week here. I think we can make an identification. A young male, five-ten or so, strong, but lanky rather than bulky, a cowboy nearing his mid-twenties."

"Great. That only describes half the county, not to mention the state."

She shrugged. "Jackson is already checking the tribal missing-persons records. I'd suggest you get someone on the county files right away. Rafe Rawlings volunteered to check the city reports."

"Rawlings was at the site, too? What was it—a damned field day?" Judd snarled.

"Only Jackson was at the site. I saw Rafe patrolling the highway and flagged him down. He's interested in forensics."

"I'll bet," Judd muttered under his breath. He wished to hell people would stay out of what should have been *his* investigation.

"If I'm keeping you from an important date, please feel free to leave," she informed him coolly. "I'll lock up when I'm through here."

She placed her precious bones in their protective covers and stored them in the cabinet he'd assigned for her use. Her bearing was as stiff as a cactus and about as friendly.

"Winona called," he said, ignoring her dismissal.

"Oh?"

A smile tugged at the corners of his mouth. She'd always gone into her cool, barely speaking mode when she was miffed at him. He knew how to get her out of a snit.

He frowned. No, he didn't. Well, he did, but he couldn't grab her up in his arms and kiss that ticklish spot on her neck until her temper collapsed into a fit of giggles, then sighs, then moans as the kiss changed....

"What did she say?"

"Who?"

"Winona."

He gave her a blank look.

She heaved an exasperated breath. "You said Winona called."

The worry came back. "She said you must have discovered more bones. She had a feeling, she said. She thinks you're in danger."

Tracy nibbled on her lower lip while she thought. He wanted to take over the task for her. He watched her, the hunger growing stronger by the second. He saw her gaze drift over his face, down his body.... She looked startled, then her eyes flicked back to his face. He gave her a sardonic smile, acknowledging the erection he couldn't hide.

"Yeah," he said softly, "I've got a feeling, too. I think I know where the danger lies." He returned her steady gaze and forced himself to warn her. "With me."

"Us," she corrected with the honesty he'd always admired in her. "The danger is between the two of us." She managed to smile, but it was rather wobbly at the edges.

He shoved a hand through his hair, frustrated by the passion that just wouldn't give up and die. To get mixed up with her again was stupid. In another week, she'd be gone. And he'd have to face the emptiness all over again.

"Yes," he finally said. "But we're adults. The attraction is there, but we don't have to act on it. You were right. It's no good between us." He paused and tried to think of something to add to that. "It's no good," he repeated.

But once it had been the best. He went to the door, aware of the utter silence in this part of the building and that they were alone. "Call Winona so she'll know you made it back all right."

"I will."

He walked out, then sat in the truck until she left. He followed at a discreet distance until she was safely home.

The police station steps were jammed with reporters, television crews, photographers and spectators when Tracy arrived at seven the next morning. Questions were tossed at Judd faster than he could answer them. He smiled when he saw Tracy.

"Here's the person you should talk to," he announced, clearing a path up the steps for Tracy. "The FBI is in charge of the case, since the bones were found on a federally designated reservation."

"You louse," she muttered under her breath as he took her elbow and led her to the columned portico.

He gave her an oblique glance and smiled that slow, sexy grin that melted the heart. "It's all yours," he said and stepped back.

Flashbulbs went off in her face. Several microphones angled through the air toward her, supported on long poles, like some kind of prehistoric octopus.

For the next half hour, she answered questions about the "cowboy" and his mysterious demise. At the end of that time, she smiled and nodded—graciously, she hoped—and headed for the door of the police station. Judd opened it for her and ushered her inside.

In the conference room, she laid her purse on a table and fell into a chair. "Now I know how celebrities must feel. That was like facing a pack of starving hyenas."

Judd brought her a cup of coffee and set it on the conference table in front of her. The corners of his mouth were curved in amusement. "Such is fame."

She made a rude face while he laughed.

"So what's next on your busy agenda?"

"The missing-persons files."

He nodded. "I've got a man assigned to work with you on that." He paused and gave her a sardonic glance. "Guess who's been assigned to the task at city hall?"

"Rafe Rawlings," she promptly surmised.

"Right."

He drank from a mug that had holly and red ribbons painted on it. A Christmas present, she assumed, and wondered who had given it to him. Not that it was any of her business, of course.

"Who do I see?" she asked.

"I'll introduce you to the officer in charge of the archives."

She spent the rest of the day reviewing the missing-persons files for a ten-year period starting twenty years ago. She was surprised at the number of people who simply disappeared, even from a small county like Whitehorn.

Where did they go? she mused. Did they lie in unmarked graves like the young cowboy they'd found?

She shook her head at the unfairness of life. She thought of the people left behind, always wondering what had happened to their loved ones, never knowing. It was bound to have a profound effect on their lives.

"Tracy?" Judd stuck his head around the door. "It's time to lock up."

She closed the last folder in the file. The missing "person" in it was a dog named Bob White. Someone had realized this after the all-points bulletin had gone out. The dog had been found, but the folder had been left in the file. Some officer had probably thought that was a nice little joke to leave around for someone like her to find years later.

"Any prospects?" Judd asked.

"Not really. Mostly it's teenage boys or men in midlife crises who take off for parts unknown, it seems."

"No women?"

"Umm, there was one that sounded interesting." Tracy rose and stretched her tired back. "A teenager named Lexine Baxter. She would be about your age now. I didn't know her, but I remember the old Baxter ranch. It was bought by the Kincaids, I think... yes, when Mr. Baxter died. His daughter had a reputation for being wild. The missing-persons report was filed by an aunt. I don't think she was very interested in finding the girl...."

She stopped as Judd smiled in his slow, sexy way.

"What?" she asked.

"You should write a book. Your childhood gave you a unique view of every family in the county, including the Cheyenne."

"You're right. I knew someone from every family who'd ever played a part in Whitehorn history. For instance, the original Baxter was a prospector looking for sapphires. Did you know that?"

"No, but I'm not surprised. Montana is known for sapphires, isn't it?"

She nodded. "I need to go back out to the site tomorrow. I want to check the soil under the ledge before it rains."

"For what?"

"Blood. Hair. Bits of material from clothing. It was getting late, and Jackson thought we should leave, so I didn't have a chance yesterday."

"Maybe he was worried about the ghosts of his ancestors getting mad about you being there," Judd suggested coolly.

"Maybe," she returned in the same tone.

He thrust a hand through the thick wave that had a tendency to fall over his forehead. "Sorry. It's been a long day... week ... month." He grinned ruefully.

She could vouch for that. The ten days she'd been there had been difficult, to say the least. She arranged the files neatly and retrieved her purse. "Well, I'm off."

"Good night," he said when she passed him.

She murmured a reply and walked swiftly from the office. Outside, she stood on the top step and looked out over the town she knew as well as Missoula, where she'd lived for the first nineteen years of her life.

A sense of being adrift came over her. She didn't feel she belonged anywhere. It was daunting to be thirty-six and feel she'd accomplished little, belonged nowhere, had no ties to the future. She'd once had such high expectations of life.

Unable to face the empty cottage, pleasant as it was, she headed for the café instead of her car. As she'd expected, Lily Mae was there.

"Tracy, come join us," the widow called across the room as soon as Tracy entered. The restaurant owner was with her, both of them drinking iced tea.

Tracy spoke, then asked, "Have you eaten?"

"Yes, but I'll stay while you eat," Lily Mae volunteered. "We've heard about the cowboy. It was all over the TV today. Tell us about it. Do you have any clues as to who he is?"

Tracy received a sympathetic smile from Melissa Avery.

"No," she replied. "We're searching the missing-persons files at present, but there're no real prospects." She repeated some of the information she'd given Judd earlier.

"I think it's terrible," Melissa said.

"Yes," Tracy agreed, thinking of the young cowboy, dying alone like that.

"Why is it mostly men who can't seem to stick with their responsibilities?" the waitress went on. "They run off and leave their wives and children all alone." She stopped abruptly. "Excuse me. I have to take care of the register."

When she left, Lily Mae leaned close. "Her father ran out on them years ago."

Tracy was at once curious. "How long ago?"

"Well, let's see, that must have been when I was married to my first husband. Yes...yes, it was."

Lily Mae counted time in three eras—husband number one, husband number two and husband number three. Was Samuel Thaddeus Roper to be husband number four?

"Melissa must be close to thirty," Lily Mae recounted. "She was just a baby when it happened."

"About thirty years? How old was her father when he left?"

Lily Mae studied Tracy, then understanding dawned in her eyes. She shook her head and leaned close again. "The bones don't belong to Charles Avery. He left town with that Baxter girl."

"Lexine?" Tracy couldn't keep the surprise from showing.

"Yes, that was the one." Lily Mae gave a disgusted grimace. "That girl was trouble from the word go, always wanting something more than she had, putting on airs and all."

Tracy wasn't interested in Lexine's sordid past. "I didn't see a missing-person report on Charles Avery."

"Well, I expect his wife was too embarrassed. Everyone knew he'd been carrying on something awful with Lexine Baxter. Then one day he climbed in his pickup and disappeared." Lily Mae leaned closer. "The cook that used to be at the Kincaid ranch—she was a cousin to my first husband, bless their souls—saw Lexine driving the truck that same day. So the whole county knew they'd taken off together. It was terrible for his wife, humiliated and left with two kids to raise..."

She shut up when Melissa joined them again and the conversation became general. After she ate, Tracy walked down the block in the evening air, which was cooling off nicely.

The story of Melissa Avery's father saddened her. People made such foolish choices, such stupid mistakes. *As she had done when she'd asked Judd for a divorce?* She didn't want to think about it.

She climbed into her car, stopped at the grocery store, then drove home. The sky was almost dark when she arrived. After putting the groceries away and changing clothes, she sat on the porch.

Deciding a walk would help her sleep, she started out. She'd gone a half block when she realized where she was heading. She kept on walking until she came to the house.

For the first time, there was a light on in the living room window and she could see inside. She stopped across the street, staying in the shadows. She waited, wanting to see the child who lived there, whether it was a little boy or girl.

The screen door slammed at the house next door to the one she and Judd had built. A boy dashed outside and peered around the yard with a flashlight. He looked to be nine or ten, a bit older than Thadd had been.

When he couldn't find what he wanted, he ran out the front gate, down the lane and through the gate next door. He went up to the front door and knocked.

The door opened. Judd stepped outside.

Tracy's heart stopped, started, skipped several beats, then pounded so hard her chest hurt. Breathing became difficult.

"Hi, Sheriff, did you see my soccer ball today? I can't find it anywhere," the boy sang out. It was obvious he and his neighbor were on comfortable terms.

"Hi, Jimmy. No, I haven't seen it since that day it was by the porch steps. When was the last time you remember using it?"

"Um...uh, I think it was day before yesterday. Me and Mike were playing in the road. I had to go in...oh, I bet he took it with him 'cause I had to go to the dentist."

"Give him a call, why don't you? Let me know if you don't find it. I'll help you look tomorrow."

"Right. Thanks. I'll call Mike now. Will you help me over the fence?"

"Sure." Judd followed his young neighbor to the rail fence, which had "cultivated" blackberries growing along it. He easily lifted the boy across the barrier and set him down on the other side.

"Thanks," Jimmy called and ran toward his house.

Judd watched him go. The streetlight illuminated his smile for a second before he turned back to his own house. He stopped suddenly and tilted his head as if listening, then he swung around.

Tracy stepped from the shadows and walked across the road. At the open gate, she hesitated, then walked through.

Judd strode to her. They stood there in the whispery soft night, the rustlings of the pine needles, the sigh of the wind from the mountains surrounding them.

"You live here?" she asked.

She hardly recognized her own voice, it was so strained. Her throat ached with emotion she couldn't allow to escape.

"Yes."

"How . . . why?"

"It came on the market a couple of years ago. I decided to buy it back."

"I see." She didn't, not really.

"It was a good buy." His tone was hard, defensive. "I always liked the location. The privacy," he added, as if this explained everything.

She got her emotions under control, even managed a smile. "It's well built. I can vouch for that. Is it . . . has it changed much . . . inside?"

He stared at her, searching her expression with a closed moodiness in his eyes. "They finished the storage room upstairs and made it into a sitting room."

"Oh. That sounds nice. I'd like to see it, if I may," she said on impulse.

She didn't need a lot of light to see the stiffness in his shoulders. *He didn't want her inside.*

That hurt.

"Sometime," she quickly added. "Maybe before I leave, you'll give me the dime tour." She laughed to show she was joking and backed up a step. "Well, I'd better go. It's late."

She turned to leave, feeling his animosity like a whiplash against her back.

"You can see it now if you'd like," he said just before she stepped through the gate.

"It's too much trouble." She faced him, wondering why he so disliked the thought of her being there.

"It's okay." He sounded resigned. He gestured for her to precede him down the path.

At the front door, he reached around her and opened it, waiting for her to go inside before he let it slam softly behind them. She gazed eagerly around the entrance area.

The hallway that led to the kitchen was paved with natural stone that had been sealed and polished. To the right was a step down into the living room; to the left was a family room. Each could be closed off from the hall by double French doors.

A television was on in the family room. Judd crossed the polished oak floors and turned it off, then closed the oak cabinets they'd built into one end of the room to hold the TV, stereo and the many books they'd accumulated.

Someone had added plaid swags over the windows, which had wooden blinds for privacy. The material matched the green-blue-and-black plaid of the sofa. A braided rug defined the sitting area. When they'd lived there as a family, they'd given Thadd's room to the grandparents when they'd visited and put Thadd on the sofa in the family room.

The living room had a blue-velvet sofa with two velvet chairs in blue-and-green stripes. The swags over those windows matched the chairs. An oriental rug picked up the colors in jewel tones.

"It's well coordinated," she remarked.

He nodded.

She drifted toward the kitchen. It stretched the width of the house. The master bedroom opened off one side of it. Both rooms had views of the ten acres of woods behind the house. Outside, a deck made a nice place for cookouts and summer entertaining.

The stairs were located between the family room and the kitchen. She went up the treads, noting the carpet. She and Judd hadn't used carpeting because she was allergic to dust. Plain floors were better for her.

The upstairs bedroom held a queen-size bed, two tables, two lamps, a rocking chair and an old-fashioned oak dresser. A telephone and note pad were conveniently placed on one of the bedside tables. The wallpaper Thadd had chosen was gone, and the walls were a creamy white. The bed cover was the only spot of color—a deep green velour blanket, soft and luxurious looking.

The storage room was gone, its door removed and widened into an arch. The bathroom between the two rooms had been enlarged to include a shower stall. Bookcases had been added to the walls around the stair landing, transforming it into an attractive foyer. The whole of the upstairs made a private retreat.

"This is very nice," she murmured. "Very nice."

"Thanks."

"Did you do it?"

"I redid the bath to add the shower. I thought it would be better... for when there was company."

She wondered what company he had. His parents. His sister and her husband and two kids. A cousin he'd once been close to and the cousin's current girlfriend. She hadn't much liked having the cousin visit. He'd had a different woman each time.

"Very nice," she repeated.

She turned and nearly ran into him. She hadn't realized he was standing quite so close, one step down from her.

Their lips were nearly on the same level. She drew a shaky breath as the tension escalated to storm intensity.

Eight

Tracy moved first. She laid her hands, both of them, flat against his chest. She wasn't trying to ward him off. It was simply that the need to caress him, to feel his warmth, was more than she could resist at this moment.

It seemed the world stood still, listening, waiting to see what would happen. She waited, too.

A glance into his eyes informed her that he was fully aware of the escalating tension between them. She saw the tendons in his neck stand out as if he fought for control.

He removed his hand from the banister.

She felt it settle lightly at her waist, large and warm and somehow comforting. She sighed shakily, knowing they were on dangerous ground, but unable to force herself to retreat.

Longing poured into the molten core of her, then spiraled outward until she felt consumed by needs she'd denied for years. A harsh pulse of desire beat its way through her veins.

"I want you," she whispered. "I—I shouldn't...but I do."

His hand tightened on her. "A person would be crazy to get mixed up in all this again," he said in a husky tone that mixed mockery with a moody anger. "I've been bitten by the spider of passion before. It's a sure bet for misery."

She lifted her palms as if stung and tried to step back.

He held her in place with both hands. "No, don't pull away. It's something that has to happen. Perhaps when this—" his glance indicated them and the passion neither could deny "—this insanity is played out, then maybe we'll be free." He gave a brief, bitter laugh. "Or maybe we're doomed to stay in this circle of hell forever."

His bitterness hurt. "Walk away," she challenged. "Walk away now, and let it be finished."

He shook his head. "It's too late." He lowered his head.

She turned her face to the side. "I don't know where this will lead . . . or where it will end." That was the scary part.

"What does it matter?" He sounded weary and defeated, as if he were as tired as she was of fighting the attraction. "It doesn't have to lead anywhere. There's just now, this moment. . . ."

She felt his breath fan over the side of her neck. They spoke without looking at each other, their heads close as if they were whispering secrets in each other's ears, but other than his hands at her waist and hers trapped between them against his chest, they didn't touch.

Invoking common sense didn't help at all, she found. Every part of her wanted what he promised—this moment and the completion it dangled before her like a long-desired gift.

He moved one hand, sliding it behind her, caressing the small of her back, exerting the tiniest bit of pressure to propel her forward.

"And then what?" she asked softly. "There's always tomorrow to be faced." Sadness boiled up in her from deep inside. She wanted more than a moment. She wanted tomorrow and the next day and the next. . . .

"Shh." His lips brushed her hair, her temple, her cheek.

She couldn't hold her lashes up. They were too heavy. She let her eyes close. He kissed them and her nose, her temple.

Against her hands, she felt his chest lift in a deep breath. A low, throaty sound of male need caressed her ears as he exhaled. Seemingly of their own volition, her hands slipped upward, removing the barrier between them. She wrapped them around his shoulders.

Flashes of heat lightning fused them together, her breasts against his chest. Willpower, good sense, caution went up in flames. She gave a little sob and sought his lips.

He positioned his head, letting her mouth touch his, then he opened his lips and gave her the kiss she yearned for.

It was as if they became locked in mortal combat. He moved his hands restlessly over her body. She did the same, striving to become closer and closer. But each new hold was ultimately unsatisfying.

There was only one closeness that would take away the painful hunger that racked them both, she realized . . . and fill the emptiness that had lived in her for years.

She moaned when his lips left hers. He kissed the hollow below her ear, then moved swiftly down her neck. He pushed her shirt collar aside and nuzzled her throat, then his hot, wet kisses burned a trail down the V opening to the first button.

He hesitated, but when she said nothing, he reached between them with one hand and flicked the button free. Then another. And another. His lips followed his hands.

At her waist, he pulled the cotton loose from her jeans. She clung to his shoulders when he slipped his hands up her back. The release of her bra caused strange sensations, like Fourth of July sparklers going off inside.

With her eyes closed, she experienced the removal of her clothing through the sense of feel—the whisper of cloth on flesh as the shirt was pushed off her shoulders and down her arms, the lighter sensation, like an echo, when he whisked the bra away.

And then the breathless anticipation as he bent his head toward her. He kissed her breasts, first one, then the other.

A shudder went through him.

She cradled his head against her and stroked through the thick, black waves of his hair, loving the tactile pleasure of touching him.

When he ran his tongue over her hardened nipple, she gasped aloud at the intense pleasure. "It's been so long," she murmured, her voice breaking as her senses were overwhelmed.

"Forever," he breathed against her. He drew spirals over her with his tongue, leaving a hot trail of moist desire behind.

He lavished attention on her breasts until she was weak in the knees. "I can't stand up," she murmured, clinging to him as her legs trembled uncontrollably.

She felt his arms close around her thighs. He lifted her from the floor, stepped up the remaining stair and proceeded into the bedroom. He laid her on the velour blanket and followed, lying half over her, his thigh nestled between hers.

"It hurts," she whispered, "to want…like this…." She moved her head restlessly back and forth against the blanket.

He slipped his hand into the hair at her temple and held her still. His eyes as he gazed into hers were haunted by visions she could only guess at. She clamped her teeth into her lower lip, wondering if he would leave her.

Then slowly... slowly... he lowered his head until their lips came together once more. She met the kiss with trembling ardor, eager for his touch. His tongue slipped between her lips, and he stroked her mouth until she responded with wanton demands of her own.

Wildfire enveloped her, and she moaned with ecstasy. He released her mouth and spoke against her lips.

"When you do that...when you moan and let me know how much you want me, it drives me to the wall, right to the wall. I want you, too, but you can tell that, can't you? A man can't hide his needs the way a woman can."

Her heart went all jumpy and nervous in her chest. She knew if they didn't stop now, they would make love...and then it would be too late to stop.

Too late?

It was already too late. A sob broke through the yearning. She felt his surprise when she wrapped her arms around him and went wild in his arms... simply wild.

She stroked and caressed with her hands and her body, moving against him until every part of her had been touched by him. She heard the whimpering demands that escaped from her parted lips and didn't care. It had been too long, much, much too long.

Through the red haze of wild hunger, she heard him murmuring to her. "Easy, love, easy. We have plenty of time, hours and hours of time."

But the fierceness that glittered from under his half-closed lashes matched the ardor that consumed her.

"Now," she demanded. "Come to me now."

He drew a ragged breath, then cupped her face with one hand and settled his lips on hers again. He moved over her, rubbing his body against hers through the clothing that separated them. She tore frantically at his shirt until she had it open. He lowered his weight on his arms until his chest pressed like a solid sheet of fire against hers.

She closed her eyes again as savage heat poured over her and held on to him as tightly as she could.

All the bright dreams of her youth rose inside her, demanding notice, seeking satisfaction. No, no, she didn't believe in those anymore...but it would be easy...so easy to fall into those gentle delusions once more...so very easy....

"You're beautiful," he murmured over and over to her. "No other woman does this to me...makes me forget everything but the moment...makes me so wild I'd die before I let you go...."

"Yes," she whispered, barely hearing his words over the roar in her ears. "Oh, please..."

When his hand settled between their bodies, she twisted to the side to give him room. He unfastened the snap and zipper of her jeans. She held her breath as he slipped a hand inside, sliding under the lace band of her French bikinis, and caressed her abdomen.

"Judd," she said with a sigh. She ran her hands under his shirt and stroked all along his back, then pulled him hard against her.

"I've dreamed of doing this," he admitted harshly. "Every minute of every day. Thoughts of you tag along with me no matter what I'm doing. I think of your skin— how smooth it is, how pale, as pale as milk, and soft...so soft."

He pushed lower, cupping her mound in his palm. He stroked her intimately, causing her to murmur and writhe as the terrible need drove her toward completion with him.

"Come to me," she demanded. "Please, love, come to me."

He took a deep breath and pushed up from her with a powerful thrust of his arms. She opened her eyes and looked at him. Their gazes locked as he stood and tossed the loosened shirt aside. His hands went to his belt, but his eyes never left hers.

She waited anxiously, afraid it was all a dream, that she was going to wake and the moment disappear.

The telephone rang instead.

They both jumped. Judd cursed, low and eloquent. He glanced at the phone in irritation.

"I have to answer," he said.

She nodded.

He picked up the instrument and spoke his name, then listened. "Yeah," he said. "I'll be there in ten minutes."

The magic evaporated. A shiver passed over her. She sat up and crossed her arms over her chest.

"There's been a bad car accident. The hospital needs blood. I have to go." He reached down, picked up his shirt and pulled it on, fastening it with angry, impatient movements.

She looked around for her own clothing.

He brought her shirt and bra to her. "Will you stay?"

His voice was so low she had to strain to hear it. She hesitated, one part of her desperately wanting to say yes, another part glad of the reprieve and a chance to regain her senses.

She shook her head. "I think I'd better go."

A stark expression flickered over his face and was gone. He nodded. "I'll drop you by your place on the way."

"Do you think...should I go to the hospital? If they need blood..." she added at his quick glance.

He shrugged. "I suppose."

She slid from the bed and, with her back to him, pulled the undergarment on. She heard his footsteps behind her, then on the stairs.

"I'll meet you at the truck," he called over his shoulder.

"Fine." She finished with her clothing and ran quickly down the steps and outside. Judd waited in the truck, the motor running, the lights on, ready to go. She ran across the lawn and climbed in.

He turned the police lights on, but not the siren as he took Route 17 to Highway 191, which ran by the county hospital.

When they reached the hospital, she saw two ambulances already at the emergency entrance. Another could be seen in the distance, coming north on the highway, its siren wailing through the night.

She followed Judd inside.

Sterling McCallum was there, talking to a doctor. When Sterling moved aside, she recognized the sharp profile of Kane Hunter. She'd known Kane on the reservation. He was a couple of years younger than she was and completely dedicated to healing.

"What happened?" Judd asked when he came abreast of the two men. He left enough room for her to join the group.

"Drag racing," Sterling replied. "The cars sideswiped. One flipped over, the other crossed the median into oncoming traffic."

"Kids," Judd concluded.

Sterling nodded. "Drinking. Whites and Indians."

Kane muttered under his breath. Tracy felt his frustration with his tribal members in particular and with youth in general. He ran an alcohol-prevention program on the reservation. "Can you guys donate some blood? We're going to need a lot."

Tracy said yes when the other two did.

"Hello, Tracy," Kane said. A smile warmed his face momentarily. "I knew you were back, but I haven't had time to look you up yet. It's good to see you again."

They had no chance to talk more. The third ambulance arrived and delivered its load of injured. Kane, head of the trauma team, went to check on a youth who looked about seventeen. Blood was all over him. A girl was helped out of the front of the vehicle. She held a compress to her head.

A hand closed over Tracy's wrist. "This way," Judd said.

A nurse took them along a corridor to another room. With quiet efficiency, she checked their vital signs, then settled them in reclining chairs rather like those in a dentist's office. In a few minutes, Tracy and the two men were hooked up.

Other people arrived as the news spread over the town grapevine. When Sterling was done, another donor took his place at once. Tracy smiled as she recognized her old friend.

"Tracy, Judd," Jackson Hawk greeted them. His dark eyes flashed from one to the other. "Everyone is turning out for the emergency, I see."

Tracy felt heat creep into her cheeks. She sensed that Jackson saw much more. She had assumed everyone in the emergency room would be too busy to notice that she'd arrived at the hospital with Judd, but that was probably wishful thinking. In a small town like Whitehorn, the hospital staff would just file the information away until they got a chance to comment on it.

When she and Judd had separated before the divorce, the news had spread like a flash fire. Telephones had started ringing minutes after he'd packed and walked out the door.

"Okay, you're finished," the nurse announced. She removed the needle, pressed cotton and a bandage over the vein and cautioned Tracy about sitting up too quickly.

When she and Judd left the room, they went into the cafeteria, where orange juice, coffee and cookies were laid out for the donors to replenish their fluids and blood sugar. Other people—family members and those who couldn't give blood—were there, too. As in the past, an emergency drew the county together.

Tracy remembered coming to this room for cup after cup of coffee while the surgical team tried to save Thadd. The town had turned out for them, too.

Several people called to them. She stopped and talked to former neighbors she hadn't seen in years. A cup of juice was pressed into her hand. She glanced into dark eyes that observed her closely, but without discernible emotion.

"Thank you," she said to Judd. She quickly drank the juice down as a slight dizziness washed over her. She wasn't sure the dizzy spell was from the drop in her blood pressure or from the way Judd looked at her. The moment passed.

When he walked off, Tracy watched him go, aware of a tug at her heartstrings. He was silent, as attentive as ever... and wary.

She understood the latter. They were daily becoming more entangled in the hot caldron of mutual desire. She was aware of him as she moved about the room, chatting with acquaintances and finally sitting to eat a piece of cake with Lily Mae Wheeler.

"That Judd," Lily Mae said in approval. "He's a rare type of man, he is." She sighed, then glanced at Tracy from the corner of her eyes. "I didn't see that little blue car you drive in the parking lot."

"I rode over with Judd," Tracy admitted, giving Lily Mae a bland, innocent look.

"Working late, weren't you?"

Tracy refrained from telling the friendly, nosy widow where to get off. "Um," she said noncommittally, not wanting to tell an outright lie. She patted back a yawn and realized how tired she was. She glanced around the crowded room.

Judd was talking to two couples, one Anglo, the other Indian. Parents of the injured teenagers, she assumed. They looked ravaged by despair and anger brought on by the helplessness of the situation. She knew the feeling.

"He's a handsome man," Lily Mae continued. "Some woman is sure to nab him soon."

Tracy forced a smile. "He's not a stray dog to be taken in and made a pet of."

"No, he's more like a mustang, smart and wary as they come. But he could be roped in by a sharp woman. He's lonely...and he's a man, the type who feels responsible for his partner. If he were lured into bed, he'd marry the woman...if that's what she wanted. Oh, there's the new teacher. Have you met her?" Lily Mae stood.

"No," Tracy said. "I think I'll head home."

She saw Sterling McCallum going toward the door. Maybe she could hitch a ride. She asked Lily Mae to tell Judd she was leaving, bade the woman good-night and rushed for the door.

"Sterling," she called, racing down the steps and across the drive to catch him before he left.

He paused at his car.

"Could I get a ride home?" She steadied herself with a hand on the vehicle. Running had made her dizzy.

"Be careful," he cautioned. "It'll take a few hours to build your blood volume back up."

"Yes, I keep forgetting. It's been awhile since I was a donor." She smiled at him. "I'm okay now. Do you have time to drop me by the cottage?"

His hesitation was brief. "Sure. Hop in." He opened the door for her.

She felt like a criminal sneaking away from the crime scene as they reached the highway and accelerated. A few minutes later he was pulling up at the cottage.

"Jessica wants to know if you'll come out for supper tomorrow night—"

"Oh, I just remembered. I'm supposed to go to Jackson's house. I've never met his wife."

"Um, I think Jessica was going to call them, too. Let me check with her."

"Okay. Thanks for the ride." She jumped out as soon as he stopped. With a wave over her shoulder, she dashed for the house.

Once inside, she locked the dead bolt behind her. She felt as if she'd just returned from combat. And was lucky to be back in one piece.

She washed and changed into her pajamas and robe, then sat on the sofa in the living room and turned the lamp off. In the dark, she contemplated the evening just past. She wasn't in one piece, she realized. She'd lost her heart to that wild mustang, the sheriff of Whitehorn County.

Tracy stood in the council office, a cup of coffee in her hand. Frank Many Horses—Uncle Frank to her—was seated at his desk. They were discussing the case.

"So you don't think the bones belonged to an Indian?" the tribal chairman asked, frowning thoughtfully at her.

"Well, I can't be positive," she admitted. "The thigh bone has a slight twist to it, which indicates Caucasian rather than Mongoloid, which usually has more of a twist. But those are generalities."

"Jackson tells me you could do DNA tests?"

She nodded.

"The parents are anxious to find out if the bones belong to their son. He disappeared fifteen years ago."

"If I can find the skull, I'll be able to tell more without running tests."

"They will pay," Frank Many Horses added. "Their son's remains, if it is their son, must have a proper burial."

"Kane can take blood samples from the parents to check against the sample from the marrow of the bones," Jackson interjected. "If you will approve the tests."

"Of course," she murmured.

She stayed another thirty minutes out of courtesy and spoke of trivialities such as the weather, which was threatening rain. Jackson accompanied her outside to her car when she left.

"Jessica called Maggie and asked if we would come to her house tonight for dinner rather than trying to have a cookout. She said Sterling had already invited you."

"Yes, he mentioned it at the hospital last night."

"Good. Sterling said to tell you Judd would pick you up this evening around seven. Okay?"

Tracy murmured that it was, but her heart was jumping around in her chest. She hadn't gone by the office this morning because she hadn't wanted to face Judd after their tempestuous episode at his house. Now she was to be his date for the evening, apparently.

And would most likely end up in his bed.

After saying her farewells, she drove out to the site and went immediately to the ledge where she and Jackson had found the thigh and hipbones. She laid out her tools—tweezers, trowel, brush, magnifying glass and a small screen nailed to a wooden frame.

She began the laborious job of sifting through the dirt. Two hours later, she wondered if this was a good idea. Her back ached, her allergies were making her eyes and nose itch and the air was hot and ever more humid.

Hearing a noise, she glanced up. The clouds were spreading over the mountains like the gathering of a witches' coven.

It made her uneasy.

She went back to work. At last, finding a suspicious patch of darker soil under the eroded end of the ledge, she took some samples. After sifting more of the dark soil through the screen, she checked the debris left on top of the sieve.

A hair.

Using the tweezers, she carefully put her find in one of the small sample bottles and stored it in her pack. When she went back to the hole under the ledge, she heard a sound like a moan. The hair stood up on the back of her neck. She glanced all around.

A rumble of thunder sounded in the distance.

She studied the cloud formations, then went back to work. A squirrel chirred loudly, then went silent, the racket broken off as if the creature had been choked.

Tracy shook her head in exasperation. Nerves. Hers were reacting to every little thing today.

With her senses acutely tuned to her surroundings, she scooped another trowel of dirt onto the wire screen and sifted it. She found a few more hairs.

Curious, she took out her magnifying glass and examined the evidence. The hairs were short, dark brown to sandy blond. Male, she concluded. Caucasian. Sun-bleached hair. A cowboy, perhaps.

Now if she could only find the skull. Teeth were the most reliable visual method of identification.

Something hit the side of her neck and slipped down her shoulder to land in her lap. A stone.

She stared at it as if she'd never seen one before, then looked up at the sky. Strong updrafts could sometimes pick up rocks and debris and deposit them miles away.

Except there was no wind blowing up the lip of the bluff.

As she turned to look back at the woods, another pebble hit her. She gasped and put a hand to her cheek. It hadn't hurt, but she was alarmed. Who was throwing rocks at her?

She stayed low as she swung around for a full view behind her. Nothing. She surveyed the woods, noting the absolute quiet.

Her heart began a fast, heavy pounding. It seemed like a warning. She clenched the sample jar as she tried to talk herself out of this foolishness.

Honestly, her imagination was running away with her. There was no danger here in the woods. She'd been working up here for days without any disturbances.

Yeah, but she was getting close to identifying the bones. And everybody in the country knew it after the TV and radio broadcasts yesterday, full of speculation about a break in the case at any time.

She was about to start back to work when a jingling sound started in the woods. Her breath caught. She forced herself to be calm.

The jingling came again, but to her left this time. She glanced that way. Then it came from the right. She swung her head around, but didn't see anything out of the ordinary.

Then the jingles started again, coming from both directions at once and increasing in volume.

Fear crawled down her back like a thousand-legged insect. Her skin seemed alive with them.

Without taking her eyes from the woods, she reached out and pulled her day pack toward her. She removed the rock pick, then slipped the container of hairs inside and zipped the pocket.

The jingling stopped all at once.

Tracy felt the silence as a threat. She got to her feet, her mind busy picking out an escape route over the rough terrain. Luckily, from her recent explorations, she knew every rock and cranny.

The bluff presented the greatest danger. The rocky outcropping was the highest point above the creek below. If she fell from there—or was pushed—the fall would kill her.

The jingling started again, first left, then right, then both. Then came laughter. Raucous and cruel, it reverberated from the rocks and trees until it seemed to surround her.

Fear flew all around her, scattering her thoughts so that she wanted to cower under the ledge and hide from the terror that stalked the woods.

Judd, help! She instinctively sent the plea out, directing it toward the town and the man who meant safety to her.

As if his spirit were suddenly there, she felt calm return. A coldness came over her. Someone was trying to frighten her, and she was letting them!

She straightened up, pushing the day pack under the ledge with her foot. She didn't want anything to trip her if she had to move fast.

When the laughter and the jingling stopped again, she was prepared. Tightening her grip on the pick, she waited, alert and ready to bolt if she had a chance, willing to fight if she had to.

The creature leapt from the trees, a living kachina from Hopi lore, not Cheyenne. So it wasn't Indians trying to frighten her away from their sacred grounds.

The person wore a wolf mask. It reminded her of a werewolf face from a Halloween costume. Wild hair cascaded down to the shoulders, hiding any natural hair. The clothing was a mixture of doeskin leggings, vest and shirt, with feathers of various sorts and other Indian paraphernalia that made no sense.

None of that scared her, but the two skinning knives, one in each hand, did. She'd seen Judd skin a deer with one of those and knew they were deadly sharp.

The monster stalked her. Tracy was aware of the cliff behind her and that the creature was trying to drive her in that direction. She edged up the egglike knob of limestone.

The monster followed, knives flashing over its head.

Lightning streaked across the sky, followed at once by a deafening blast of thunder. The creature started and seemed to cringe for a moment. Tracy grabbed the chance.

She bolted down the far side of the limestone slope and ran for the woods. She didn't look back. Heart pounding, she dodged among the trees, leapt over bushes and small boulders and found a path that led downward. She raced flat out along it until she came to the trail that led to her car.

Running a hand over her jeans, she felt the car keys tucked safely in her pocket. Thank God.

When she reached the clearing, she was relieved to see it empty except for her blue compact auto. She unlocked it,

jumped in and locked the door. Her hands shook as she
turned the key. The engine caught. She backed up without looking, then went forward, turning the wheel desperately. She took off in a spray of gravel and dust.

Behind her, a wild-maned, horrible-faced monster leapt
out of the woods as she turned the car to head down the
steep hill. The creature ran toward her, then threw one of
the knives at the car.

The knife hit the rear window and skidded off onto the
ground. Tracy plunged the accelerator to the floor.

"Judd, Judd," she whispered, a litany of safety in a
world gone berserk.

Nine

Judd answered the telephone on the second ring. "Hensley."

A strained gasp came from the other end. "Judd...help Tracy," someone said.

He didn't recognize the voice. "Who is this?"

"Tracy...find Tracy...danger..."

"Winona?" he asked. Fear slapped against his spine like a wet rag. He glanced at the calendar. Friday, the thirteenth.

"Yes...danger...find her..."

He realized Winona was having one of her visions. She was fighting the trancelike state in order to call him.

"I will," he promised. "I'll find her."

"Hurry...wolf after her...running...wolf..."

"Winona, rest now," he said sternly, worried about the old woman's heart. "I'll find her. Don't worry."

"Yes...go...*go!*" She hung up.

Feeling like the hounds of hell were after him, he grabbed up his holster and belted it on his hips, then checked the clip in his gun. He selected several rounds of ammunition and a rifle out of a cabinet. Then he was off.

In the car, driving on the highway toward the reservation, he called Sterling and told him to get his butt over there. He wanted backup on the case, but he wasn't going to broadcast an all-points bulletin on the basis of a psychic's vision.

He'd hardly gone a mile from town when he spied a blue car coming from the opposite direction. It was doing at least ninety. He turned across the median and headed after the speeding vehicle.

After hitting the button to start the blue lights flashing, he pushed the pedal down. While he caught up with the small car, he called Sterling and told him Tracy was all right. He pulled up beside her and blew the horn.

Her face wore a startled look as she glanced out the window. Then she recognized him. She slowed at once, then pulled to the side of the road. She was out of the car and racing toward him before he'd opened his door and slid out.

Then she was in his arms. "Judd, thank God. Oh, thank God!"

He inhaled the sweet essence of her, felt the impact of her slender body in every cell in his. "Tell me what frightened you," he murmured in a soothing tone.

"A monster . . . a wolf—"

His low imprecation interrupted her as he recalled Winona's vision. "Go on," he ordered. He thought of Rafe Rawlings, the "Wolf Boy" who was now a policeman and asking a lot of questions. But he was much too young to be involved. "You were at the site on the reservation?"

"Yes." She took a deep breath and pulled away, looking embarrassed after her show of emotion. "I was sifting through the dirt under the ledge . . . where Jackson and I found the femur and pelvis?"

He nodded, indicating he understood where she meant.

She brushed a stray lock of hair back from her temple, leaving a smidgen of dirt there. "I thought I heard something, but then it thundered, and I realized we were in for a rain, so I went back to work. Then a rock hit me—actually, a pebble—then another."

A rock! Judd felt the crystal clarity coming over him. Winona had seen a rock hitting someone in her vision. Someone had thrown a rock at Tracy....

"Then this jingling started... like jingle bells used on sleighs or something."

"The Indians use bells in their dances," he reminded her.

She nodded, then licked her lips. "The bells seemed to come from two different directions. Then the laughter started."

Anger steeled over Judd—anger so cold it chilled his blood. When Tracy came to the part about the apparition with the knives, rage enveloped his senses, shutting out everything but the need to find the person who had frightened her.

"I left my knapsack," she ended, dismayed at its loss.

"I'll get you another," he promised absently, his mind going over all he knew of the case.

"It isn't that," she said impatiently. "I had found more evidence—several short hairs, probably belonging to the victim, *and* one long one—blond... with dark roots."

He almost smiled at the dramatic pauses she used to emphasize her find.

"I left them in the knapsack," she concluded. "I need to go back and get it before—" She broke off abruptly.

"Before the wolf monster destroys it?"

She nodded.

He shook his head. Thunder rumbled over the mountains. "You go home. I'll go back and get your things."

"You can't go alone. It's too dangerous."

"I put in a call to Sterling before I found you and told him to meet me at the bluff," he said, neglecting to tell her he'd cancelled it. "By the way, I ought to give you a ticket. You must have been going ninety when I spotted you."

"Well, actually, ninety-five. I'd slowed down some because of the traffic before I saw you." She gave him an insouciant grin.

He wanted to kiss her. "Get on home before the rain starts. I'll see you around seven tonight."

"Right." She returned to her car and drove off at a sedate speed while he watched.

Solemn, he climbed back in his truck and made a U-turn across the median again. He wanted to check out the site as soon as possible.

He thought of calling Sterling, then decided against it. The poor slob had been working overtime and was supposed to be off duty that afternoon. The detective needed some time with his wife and child.

At the reservation, Judd followed the road up to the bluff, parked and climbed out. He checked the area. The skinning knife that had been thrown at Tracy was gone. He'd figured it would be.

Using the tracking skills he'd learned since living in Montana, he quietly slipped into the woods. He picked up the tracks of two people. Tracy's he recognized by the print of her sneaker soles. The other tracks were indistinct. Moccasins, he deduced. He studied one clear print. Large. A man.

The cold settled in his soul. Someone had tried to hurt Tracy. He wanted his blood.

He followed the trail upward, found the deer path Tracy had followed. He could almost feel her fear as she'd run for her life. Thank God she hadn't tried to stand her ground. A sane person had no chance against a madman.

The woods were silent, just as Tracy had described. Judd's senses were so acute he could identify the faint rustling of the leaves as the wind moved in from the west. He sniffed the air. Ozone. The storm was approaching.

Near where the woods opened on the limestone knob, he found tracks around a shrub. Examining the bush, he saw a broken branch and found a piece of string. Here was where one set of bells had been tied, he deduced.

Moving on up, he left the trees and stooped by the ledge after surveying the area. Tracy's knapsack wasn't there. He spied it several feet away... or what was left of it.

The canvas tote had been slashed into ribbons. The tools of her trade were scattered about. The sample bottles had been smashed to smithereens, their evidence lost, the hairs probably blown away by the rising wind.

The coldness inside him became glacial fury as he thought of what might have happened to Tracy had she not had the sense to run.

He followed the trail of footprints to a second shrub next to the bluff. He could easily see where something—more bells, he assumed—had been torn from a mangled branch.

The creature had been careful to take all evidence with it. A cunning monster, Judd thought.

After glancing around, he stood and looked out at the lush pasture fifty feet below. The tribe had refused to renew the lease with the Kincaids, who'd used the pasture for a hundred years. There'd been trouble brewing over the situation until Jackson's wife, Maggie, had testified before Congress. The ranchers had backed down, but they hadn't been happy.

He tried to figure out if this had any bearing on Tracy's fright, but couldn't see that it did. And she didn't think an Indian had been the culprit.

"After all, a Cheyenne should know his own culture," she'd said, rather indignant that the person hadn't dressed correctly.

A slight smile tugged at his mouth. That was Trace, a nitpicker for authentic detail. She'd learned that from her father.

The smile disappeared. He'd loved being a part of her family. They'd taken him into their closeness and kept him there. Even after the divorce, her mother had sent him gifts at Christmas and his birthday. She'd enclosed notes, too, but she'd never mentioned her daughter.

Somehow he felt he'd let go too easily. Maybe he should have confronted Tracy or fought harder for her.

But a man could only do what he could do. At the time of the divorce, he'd felt it was the only way to go. Now he wasn't so sure. There were still feelings between them. He just didn't know what the hell they were.

Well, back to the case at hand.

Before he could turn and head for the truck, something hit the back of his knee. His left leg buckled.

He tried to catch himself, but slipped on a loose piece of limestone, which flew outward as his weight slammed down on it. The shard of rock fell down the bluff. Judd realized he was going to follow it.

Instinct had him clutching the shrub desperately. It held for a second, but not long enough for him to get a toehold in the rough stone. The branch separated from the bush, and he plunged over the side....

Down, down, down, it was a long way down. He remembered the line from a book he used to read to Thadd. Dr. Seuss.

Then he started thinking about how the hell he was going to survive the fall. Maybe he'd land in the creek—one of the deep quiet pools where he and Tracy used to bathe the summer they fell in love.

He caught the stub of a dwarf tree growing from a crevice. It bent flat to the rock face with his weight, but it held.

Not for long.

When the stumpy tree started coming out by the roots, he wedged his hand in a crevice and held on while he felt around for places to put his feet. The rocky wall was shale here, loose stuff that wouldn't hold him. He felt a moment's despair as the tree slowly pulled free from the crack.

The last root gave way. He lost his grip on the narrow crevice. Then he was falling...falling.... His last thought was to wonder how Winona's goats had gotten up on the bluff.

Tracy reached for the telephone, then drew back. She glanced at the clock—7:10. Judd was late. Should she call and remind him?

What if Sterling had forgotten to tell him to pick her up? No, Judd had said he'd see her around seven. But maybe he hadn't realized he was supposed to stop for her. She'd leave...but she didn't know where Sterling and Jessica lived.

Jessica had called and confirmed that the dinner was to be at their house. Jackson and his wife would be there, too. "Jackson is going to do fry bread, and I got honey from Winona today. It's casual, so wear something comfortable."

Tracy paced to the front door and stared out at the evening sky. Where was Judd?

She chewed on her lower lip. He'd promised to retrieve her knapsack, with her tools and the evidence in it. Sterling was supposed to meet him at the site. But what if something had happened and Sterling had been delayed? Or hadn't shown up?

No, she was being silly. One thing she knew for sure—Judd could take care of himself. He was careful and alert.

A vision of the wolf-faced monster came to her.

She shivered as her fear increased a notch. She'd call Jessica and find out what time Sterling had gotten home. That was the sensible thing to do. It was stupid to stand around stewing over nothing. She crossed the room and dialed the number.

"Jessica? This is Tracy," she said when her hostess answered. "I, uh, was wondering—has Sterling gotten home yet?"

"He's been home all afternoon," Jessica said. "What's happening? Hasn't Judd stopped for you yet?"

"No. I wanted to check with you that he knew he was supposed to pick me up."

"He did. I reminded him when he called to tell Sterling to forget meeting him at the reservation."

Fear clutched at Tracy. "He told Sterling not to meet him?"

"Yes. He said he'd found you." Jessica laughed softly. "He was one worried man until then."

"Jessica, Judd went out to the site after leaving me," Tracy said, her own worry apparent in her voice. "Now he's late."

"And Judd is never late. Hold on."

Tracy heard Jessica calling to her husband. She heard Sterling's baritone voice as he joined his wife. Jessica told him what had happened.

"Tracy," he said into the phone. "The old man hasn't shown up, huh?"

"No. He was going to check out the person who frightened me. I thought you were going to meet him. It's dangerous. I've got to go—"

"Whoa, there. Tell me exactly what happened. He didn't mention any of this."

Tracy explained as quickly as she could. "I'm going out there," she added.

"Stay put," Sterling ordered. "I'll handle it."

When they hung up, Tracy ran to the bedroom and changed to jeans and a shirt, thick socks and her sturdy boots. She grabbed a raincoat and a flashlight, switching it on to make sure it worked. It did. She rushed out.

The rain was coming down in a steady drizzle as she retraced her path along the highway and onto the reservation. Sterling's truck was at the bluff when she arrived. She parked beside it and slid out. She decided she didn't need the flashlight yet.

Ducking under the police tape, she sped along the deer track to the ledge under the limestone. There she found her knapsack torn to shreds. She felt sick with worry.

What if the monster had attacked Judd? Killed him?

She saw a shadow among the trees and hid behind a boulder.

"It's me," Sterling said. He came to her. "Did you see anything on the way up?"

"No." She showed him her slashed tote. "Look."

"Damn," he said. He bent to the ground.

She flicked her light on and held it so it would highlight any footprints.

"He was here," Sterling said. "This way."

They walked to a steep section of the bluff, found the broken limb on the shrub and followed skid marks over the ledge.

Sterling lifted a large, round rock, examined it, then put it down. Tracy noted there was no depression in the dirt under it. The detective peered at the edge of the bluff. The place where the fractured chip had given way was obvious. When he looked up, he gave her a probing glance.

"I'm all right," she said, knowing that Judd must have gone over the side. "How do we get down?"

"We'll take the main road. It's faster than the dirt trail. Stay close to me. I'll have my siren on."

Clutching the steering wheel of her car, she rode the bumper of the unmarked police vehicle. Its wail reminded her of a scream in the gathering dusk when Sterling used it to clear a path through the traffic. They followed a paved county road, then a short dirt track, then no road at all as they drove across a meadow. She stopped when he did.

"We'll have to walk from here," he said.

They jogged along the creek on a path worn through the grass and underbrush by generations of fishermen.

Tracy had gone through so many emotions on the drive that she felt numb as they searched along the base of the bluff.

"We're near where he went over. I'm going across to the other side," Sterling told her. "Stay close to the creek. Start calling. He may hear."

If he's conscious. If he's alive.

"All right." She waded through the twilight as if she walked through a strange medium, thick and cloying, instead of air. Each breath burned her throat as she ignored a need to cry.

"Judd," she called softly, over and over. She was afraid her voice would alert the madman who'd tried to kill her, if he was still around. Sterling didn't seem to think he was.

She skirted a section of high boulders, pushed into their present disorder by glaciers from long ago, she decided inanely as she searched. "Judd," she called, a bit more desperately.

"Here."

She stopped, listened. Nothing. "Judd?"

"Here."

"Where? Keep talking," she ordered. His voice had been so low and weak. Fear crawled along her spine. "Judd?"

"Here."

She found him lying on the bank between two boulders. One foot still in the water, as if the effort to pull it out had been too much for him. When she touched him, his skin was cold.

"You'll catch pneumonia," she murmured.

"Yeah. The water's cold."

She ran one hand over him while she held the light with the other. She couldn't find any injuries. "You fell from the cliff?"

"Yes. Caught a bush...but it wouldn't hold." He was plainly irritated by this fact. "A damned goat sneaked up on me."

She'd thought he was lucid until this last statement. Now she realized he must be delirious. "Don't try to talk," she soothed. "Save your strength."

"Trace, be careful. Winona said you were in danger." He pushed himself up on his elbows and glanced all around.

Tears filled her eyes as she realized he was concerned for her. "I'll be careful. Sterling is with me."

"Good," he muttered. "That's good."

She straightened and cupped her hands around her mouth. "Sterling!" she yelled as loudly as she could. She waved the flashlight in the air. "I've found him."

"Coming," he called at once.

She stripped out of her rain jacket and laid it over Judd. The drizzle went right through her shirt. "Hurry," she shouted.

"I'm here." He spoke near her, startling her.

"Thank God," she said. "He's hurt. I don't know how bad." Training the light on Judd, she waited while the detective pulled him onto the path and checked him over.

"His leg is broken. I'll make a splint. Then we'll get him to the hospital."

He found a stick and secured it to Judd's leg with their belts. They were going to carry him, but Judd insisted he could walk. After making a rude sound, Sterling lifted his boss to his feet. Tracy swung one of Judd's arms over her shoulder while Sterling did the same. They headed for the road where the vehicles were parked. It seemed to take forever.

Tracy's shoulders were burning by the time they hoisted Judd into Sterling's cruiser. The detective gave Tracy her coat and tucked a blanket around the patient.

"Follow me," Sterling ordered.

Reluctantly, she left Judd and got into her car.

They arrived at the hospital in record time. The nurse recognized her when she entered the emergency room and joined Sterling. The woman smiled reassuringly, then bent over Judd.

The trauma team on duty that night checked him over, then wheeled him into a curtained area. They were teasing Judd about taking a dip in the creek at his age. Tracy wished they'd get on with it. She'd seen the paleness of his skin despite his tan.

Sterling went to call Jessica to let her know what had happened. By the time Judd was taken to have his leg set in a cast, Jessica as well as Jackson and Maggie Hawk had arrived, Jessica after first dropping Jennifer at a sitter's. Lily Mae breezed in hot on their heels.

"I listen to the police band," she explained when Tracy stared at her in surprise. "I brought you some soup."

"Thank you, but I couldn't eat," Tracy said. She had no time for food now, not when Judd was hurt.

"For later." Lily Mae brought coffee and forced Tracy to drink it. "You're wet clear through, child," the widow scolded.

Tracy thanked her for her care. "I'd better call Winona," she murmured, feeling as if she needed to talk to her friend. She borrowed some money and went to the pay phone by the door.

Winona answered on the first ring. "Tracy?"

"Yes." Tracy told her what had happened.

"I saw the wolf," Winona said in confirmation, "and called Judd. I knew you were in danger and needed him."

"He's hurt because of me." Tracy was guilt stricken.

"No, because of some crazy person who's committed a crime and doesn't want to be discovered," Winona corrected. "Take care of him. He needs you."

Tracy swallowed as emotion tightened her throat. "I will," she promised solemnly. "I owe him."

Winona chuckled suddenly. "You may pay more than you mean to." She said good-night and hung up.

Tracy returned to the hospital cafeteria and joined the others. Lily Mae had gone to visit a patient. She'd left a container of soup with Jessica to give to Tracy.

Another patrol car arrived. Rafe Rawlings got out and came inside. "How is he?" he inquired of Sterling.

"He has a broken leg. That's all we know."

Kane Hunter entered through the hallway leading to the emergency room. "He's fine, grouchy as a spring bear and demanding to go home. He's had a painkiller and is a little groggy right now. Who's going to baby-sit him tonight?"

"I am," Tracy said.

Several pairs of eyes turned to her. Sterling nodded. "Good idea," he said. A smile appeared on the tough detective's mouth. "I'll help you get him home. His place or yours?"

The question was so suggestive—and Sterling, the rat, knew it—that Tracy blushed. Jessica frowned at her grinning husband. Maggie did the same with hers.

"Jessica, your dinner!" Tracy exclaimed, remembering suddenly. "It's ruined."

"Now don't you worry about that," the other woman soothed. "I'll bring you a plate over in a little while."

"I have the fry bread in the car," Jackson stated.

It ended that the two men took Judd home in the patrol car. At the house, they dressed him in pajamas, and put him to bed while Tracy found coffee in the kitchen and put on a pot.

Jessica and Maggie brought over the food, which consisted of Brunswick stew, plus a salad and dinner rolls.

"Do you feel like eating?" Tracy asked Judd, going into the master bedroom a few minutes later.

"Yes. I don't need a baby-sitter. Kane is worse than a mother hen. Tell everyone to leave."

"That wouldn't be polite. We're having dinner here."

She glanced around the bedroom as they talked. The furniture was made of golden oak. It had belonged to Judd before they were married. His parents had given it to him.

The room was the same as when they'd lived there. Even the family picture of Thadd, Judd and her hung on the wall in its usual place near the dresser.

"I looked for that," she said. "When I left."

"I took it to the office."

Their eyes locked for a long minute. She sensed the questions that neither of them could voice. It was too soon. The attraction between them was too compelling to ignore, but the old hurts were still too raw to examine at present.

She switched to a safer subject. "Were you injured anywhere besides your leg?"

"Some scrapes. Nothing major. The break was clean. It should heal without a problem." He glanced at his palms.

"Good." She moved closer and looked at them, too. "Oh, Judd, your hands."

The gouges weren't deep, but they were extensive. Kane had cleaned them with an antibiotic and sprayed on a medical coating of synthetic skin until Judd's own could grow back.

"How did you happen to fall?" she asked.

"Damned if I know," he responded with a grouchy frown. "I thought one of Winona's goats butted me in the back of my bad knee. Crazy." He shook his head.

"Not so crazy," Sterling corrected, coming in with a tray. "Someone could have hit you in the leg. I noticed a round rock there where the skid marks were—a hefty one about four inches in diameter. That would have done the trick."

Tracy recalled the rock that hadn't made an impression in the dirt, which indicated it hadn't been in that spot long.

"But why?" Jessica came in with a cup of coffee for Judd.

Jackson and Maggie joined them. Soon they were all sitting in the bedroom, eating their supper and discussing the case.

"Does this mean someone is afraid of the bones?" Maggie asked.

Everyone looked at her.

"You know, like if we find out who the bones belonged to, then we'd know who killed the person?"

"It must be someone local, someone still here," Jessica said, "someone who doesn't want to be discovered."

"Kane said something." Sterling paused and studied Tracy. "He said there's a hermit who roams the area, a man named Homer Gilmore. He's harmless, but he does look rather weird—long, gray hair that sticks out around his head, sharp facial features. He prospects around in the hills. He has been known to scare the life out of unsuspecting backpackers."

"It wasn't an old man," she said. "Not unless he was dressed in a variety of Indian clothes and something that looked like a Halloween mask with a werewolf face, plus a wig made out of buffalo hide. It was . . . very strange."

"To say the least," Jessica agreed. "To scare someone that way—the knives and all—was a terrible thing to do."

"The person may have meant to do more than scare Tracy." Judd scowled with visible anger. "He threw a knife at her."

"Well, at my car," she corrected with a faint smile. "I don't know that he was trying to actually hit me."

Sterling gave the three women a stern raking with his dark eyes. "When someone has a weapon, you always assume he means to kill you. Always, got that?"

"Right," Judd declared.

"Absolutely," Jackson stated unequivocally.

The three women looked at the three fierce, unsmiling men. They nodded solemnly.

Tracy studied the convivial group. A feeling of peace descended over her, in spite of the day's odd, dangerous events. She was among friends. She felt as if she'd come home.

A welter of emotions washed over her, destroying the brief contentment. Yearning so painful she had to clench her teeth to hold it back rose to her throat.

She looked at the two married couples, then at Judd. Once they had been like that—happy and in love. Once… She wanted it again.

Ten

"Call if you need anything," Maggie told Tracy as she and Jackson left the house. "I'll talk to you soon."

Tracy waved to the couple, then closed the door. It had been a pleasant evening. Even Judd, in spite of his painful leg, had laughed and chatted with ease.

He and Sterling McCallum were cut from the same cloth, she thought. Jackson was more open. Or maybe he seemed that way because she'd known him most of her life.

She poured a glass of water, glanced around the kitchen, which the three women had cleaned, then returned to the master bedroom.

"Where are the painkillers Kane gave you?" she asked.

"Who said he did?" Judd challenged. "Besides, I don't need anything for pain. I feel fine. You can go home."

She ignored his dismissal and rummaged through his damp clothing, which was hanging in the bathroom. She found several packets of pills. She opened one, dumped the two tablets on her palm and carried them to him with the water.

"I can tell you're hurting," she said softly.

"You can read minds?" he demanded. "Even Winona can't do that. You two should go into business together."

"Don't be a goose," she reprimanded mildly. "You get a tense look around the eyes when you're in pain." She held out the pills.

He snorted, threw the tablets into his mouth, took the glass and swallowed the medicine in one gulp. He finished off the water and set the glass on the lamp table. "There, all gone."

"Good. Do you want to sleep or shall I read to you?"

"Neither," he said, giving her a sour glance. "You can go."

"I'm spending the night."

"Like hell!"

"It might come to that." She grinned at him, feeling very much in control. He could hardly get up and throw her out . . . well, knowing Judd, he probably could, but he wouldn't.

He took a deep breath. "Look, I appreciate your TLC, but I'm all right. Really. You don't have to play nurse."

"I'm staying." She took his wet clothing from the bathroom and went to the laundry room, which was right off the kitchen. She tossed the clothes in the tub, saw a basket of other items, sorted them, added them to the load and started the machine.

While she checked the refrigerator and started a grocery list, she wondered if he did his own cooking and cleaning. Tomorrow she would bring over food from her place.

Hmm, perhaps she'd better go tonight. She needed her pajamas and toiletries.

She realized she was planning on staying for more than the night. But maybe not. There had been wariness and resentment in Judd's eyes whenever he'd looked her way during the evening.

Sighing, she rubbed the slight tension headache that had settled in the back of her skull and considered what to do. Well, she'd stay until Judd was up and about. Kane had said he'd drop off a pair of crutches in the morning.

With that off her mind, she checked on Judd, found him asleep or pretending to be, and left the house. At the cottage, she loaded up bags with groceries and packed a change of clothing along with her pj's and ditty bag. She returned to Judd's home.

When she went in the front door, she heard him cursing in the bedroom. She dropped her stuff on the sofa and rushed to the back of the house.

She found him hanging on to a chair with one hand and the wall with the other. "What are you doing?" she cried, angry that he would take a chance on hurting himself.

"Going to the bathroom. The damned floor seems to be bucking like a mustang," he complained. "I thought you'd left."

"I went to get my things. Here." She slipped an arm around his lean waist and drew his arm over her shoulder. "Come on."

He hopped while she steadied him. They reached the bathroom. She let him go and waited. He glared at her. "Waiting for the peep show? The admission is two dollars."

Heat flared in her face at his rude remark. "I've seen it all before. For free." She flounced out.

"It was never free," he muttered. "Woman always cost men a hell of a lot."

She closed the door, ignoring the sarcastic remark. Going to the bed, she fluffed up the pillows and straightened the covers, folding the sheet down so that all would be ready when he returned.

When the door opened, she hurried across the room and offered him her arm to lean on. He accepted her aid without a word.

"Thanks," he said when she pulled the sheet over him. "I'm sorry I snapped earlier."

She was surprised at his apology. Peering at his face, she saw that his eyes were closed, his brows bunched in an unconscious grimace of weariness. Her heart went out to him.

After turning the light low, she went to the guest room, made up the bed with sheets she found in the hall closet and changed into her pajamas and robe. She washed up and returned to his room.

Choosing a comfortable chair, she sat in it and watched the drizzle run down the windowpanes in zigzag lines. She sighed and wished she could see into the future. She very much wanted to know what tomorrow would bring.

"Trace."

She opened her eyes, realized where she was and sat up straight. Judd was restless on the bed. He said her name again, this time louder and in a worried tone. She went to him.

"I'm here," she said softly.

He opened his eyes and stared at her. "Be careful," he warned. "There's danger."

"I'm okay. I'm here with you," she reminded him.

She saw comprehension dawn in his eyes. He flicked a quick gaze over the room, sizing up the situation in that swift way he had. "I remember," he said. "I was dreaming."

"Yes." She checked the clock, then got more water from the bathroom and opened another packet of pills. "Here, you can take two more of these now. I think you need them."

"My eyes tense again?"

When she glanced up at the taunting remark, she saw the wicked light in his eyes. "You must be feeling better if you're up to teasing," she murmured, pleased.

"I feel like hell," he admitted. "My leg is throbbing and itching at the same time."

"I'll rub it," she volunteered.

After he swallowed the medicine and set the glass aside, she pulled back the sheet and pushed his pajama leg up. "Lucky for you, you landed in a pool," she told him.

"Not so lucky. I kicked out from the cliff in order to hit the deep part of the creek. If I'd been just another foot over, I wouldn't have hit a rock and broken my leg."

"Umm," she crooned sympathetically. She rubbed his toes, avoiding the areas that were a nice shade of purple. When she moved above the cast to his knee, he grunted as if her touch hurt.

"Sore there," he said when she looked at him.

"Let me see." She checked the back of his knee. "You have a bruise here, too. That rock on the bluff—remember, you thought one of Winona's goats had hit you? But it must have been the rock Sterling found."

"Yeah, I remember." He stopped her hands when she slid them under the pajama material and massaged his thigh. "You'll have me hurting someplace else if you keep that up."

"Huh," she said skeptically.

"My powers of recuperation are remarkable."

"They must be if you're up to bragging so soon after your fall." She spoke with some asperity.

He smiled slightly and lay against the pillows with his eyes closed while she rubbed his toes again.

"Tonight was fun, wasn't it?" she said a few minutes later. "It's nice to have friends."

"Don't you have any friends in California?"

"Yes, but..." She couldn't tell him it was different being part of a couple and sharing things with other couples, rather than a single as she was in her other life . . . her *real* life.

She let his foot go and covered him with the sheet. Sitting in the chair, she reminded herself that she was living in a fool's world to think of herself and Judd as a couple again.

"But?" he prodded when she was silent.

"Do you ever wish we could start over?" She bit down on her lip, but the words were out.

He met her gaze. "Yeah. But I know better. I'm not going to get mixed up with you again." He shifted about until he found a more comfortable position. "What would be the use? You'll be leaving in a few days."

She had nothing to say to that.

The next morning Tracy was awake shortly after dawn. She leapt up, washed and dressed, then went to check on her patient.

Judd was asleep. Normally, he was the one up at the first light of day. She noticed he'd put a pillow under the cast. That should help keep the swelling down and relieve the throbbing.

She went to the kitchen and put on a pot of coffee, then decided on pancakes and sausage for breakfast. It was one of Judd's favorite meals.

A frown replaced the smile she'd been wearing. It was no good falling back into old routines. Judd had made his feelings plain last night. But he still wanted her.

Putting off useless brooding, she prepared the food, then left the plates in the warmed oven. When she peeked in his room, he was getting out of bed. She dashed across the room.

"Let me help." She looped his arm over her shoulders.

He sighed audibly and held on as he awkwardly walked on the thick cast. She saw him grimace, but he didn't complain.

When he was finished in the bathroom, she helped him back to bed and propped his foot on the pillow again. "I have breakfast ready. Would you like to eat now?"

When he said yes, she prepared a tray and brought it to him in bed. She found a TV tray in the family room and used it for herself. They ate in companionable silence.

At nine the calls started—local people checking on their sheriff. She screened them for him, feeling slightly jealous when he spoke to Maris—who was safely married, Tracy reminded herself.

He chatted with the rancher for several minutes before hanging up. It was obvious they were good friends and at ease with each other. He laughed more than once during the conversation.

Tracy went to the kitchen and poured them each another cup of coffee, then washed the pot. For a long time she gazed out the window at the woods. Next door, she saw the little boy—Jimmy?—and a friend playing near the trees.

She didn't look around when Judd thumped into the room.

He got his cup and stood beside her, drinking the coffee, which she'd made strong, the way he liked it. Gourmet coffee had been one of the small luxuries they'd indulged in as a newly married and very broke young couple.

"How old is your neighbor?" she asked.

"Jimmy is nine. That's his best buddy, Mark, who lives one block west of us. They'll be in fourth grade when school starts."

"You seem to know them well."

"Jimmy and I are pals. His parents are divorced. I'm sort of the regular male in his life. He helps me mow the yard and cut wood for winter."

"I see." Her voice quivered. She felt as if her heart were being torn out by the roots.

"Life does go on," Judd said harshly. He took his cup and went back to the bedroom.

"I know," she said to the empty kitchen, feeling alone and uncertain, and sure she was headed for heartbreak all over again.

Luckily, Kane Hunter showed up before she got into a serious case of self-pity. She welcomed him with a bright smile.

"Good morning, Dr. Hunter," she said in greeting.

"What's with the doctor business?" he demanded. He set a pair of crutches in the corner next to the pantry. "You and Jackson used to call me a little devil when I barged in on your games back at the res twenty or so years ago."

"All is forgiven," she assured him. "Coffee? I was just about to put on a fresh pot."

"Thanks, that would be nice. How's the patient?"

"Grouchy, but up and about. Go see for yourself."

Kane laughed and headed for the master bedroom with the crutches. She heard the men talking amiably while she waited for the coffee to finish. Judd's deeper voice ran over her ragged nerves like honey over a hot, buttered biscuit.

She suddenly remembered lazy mornings in bed, Thadd tucked between them while Judd read the funnies. She shook her head hopelessly. Remembering was *not* getting on with life.

After pouring the coffee, she took a cup to Kane and stayed while they concluded their conversation. When the doctor left, she asked Judd if she could do anything for him. "Run errands or something?" she suggested.

"Eager to be off?" he questioned, his dark gaze opaque as he studied her.

She realized she was nervously pleating and smoothing her slacks across her thigh. She forced her hands to be still. "Not particularly. If you don't need anything, I thought I would do some work."

"You should wind up the case soon, then you can leave."

"Yes."

They looked at each other. She felt herself being drawn into the dark vortex of desire he usually kept concealed. His gaze roamed over her hungrily. Her heart leapt as heat rioted through her entire body. She knew she would go to him if he but beckoned.

Before she gave in to that tempestuous yearning, she wanted one thing clarified between them. She hesitated, then gathered her courage. "Judd, when we married..."

His face took on a hard edge.

She doggedly persevered. "Was it... did you marry me because I was pregnant?"

He muttered an imprecation that shocked her.

"You never said..." She gestured helplessly. "It's something I've wondered about for a long time."

"Is that what you think?" he demanded harshly.

"I don't know." She faced him. "I don't know what I think, not anymore. You were always a quiet person. I assumed you felt the same as I did, but later, I decided I was wrong...."

He grabbed the crutches and got out of bed. He hobbled to the door, then stopped and gestured to indicate the house around them. "I built this house for you. Maybe you ought to think about why a man would do that for a woman." He stomped out, his *step-thump* mode of walking filled with anger.

Tracy let out a shaky breath. Maybe he had loved her as she'd loved him, but he didn't now. He wanted her, yes...and was furious with both of them for it.

Judd walked out on the front porch. He cursed fate for bringing Tracy back to Whitehorn. He cursed her for doubting his motives and himself for caring what she thought.

What the hell did it matter now?

He sighed as the anger cooled. What did anything matter anymore? Nothing had for a long time...at least, it hadn't until Tracy had returned, stirring up old memories he'd thought were dead, making him ache for her again.

All last night he'd thought of her in the house, sleeping only a few feet away in the chair or in the guest room. He'd awakened often and knew he'd been dreaming of her and him. Together. Making love.

A groan pushed its way out of his throat. He wanted her right now with a harsh need that drove all common sense from his mind.

And she wanted him.

He'd seen it in her eyes, the need...and the fear. She was afraid to come to him. Once she'd given herself to him with no doubts, no questions at all. She'd poured her pure, sweet love over him with no holding back.

He would have hung the moon for her if she'd asked. But she hadn't asked that. She'd asked him how to stop hurting. He'd had no answer to that question.

Moisture stung his eyes. He brushed it away impatiently. It was crazy to get involved. He wouldn't go through the pain again when she left.

Going inside, he called Sterling. "You're in charge. Contact the tribal police and go over the site with a fine-tooth comb. Tracy found some hairs. Sift through the dirt under the ledge and see if you can find some more. Bring in her pack and check it."

"Everything's under control. Jackson and I have men out there now," Sterling told him. "When will you be on your feet?"

"Kane brought me some crutches, so I'm mobile. I'll be at the office Monday. Try not to mess up in the meantime."

"I'll do my best," the detective promised. "Well, gotta go. There's trouble between the Kincaid ranch and the res. Jackson says they found Kincaid cattle in the pasture the ranch used to lease from the tribe. I'm going out to talk to Dugin now."

"Good. Then what?"

"After that we're planning a raid on the mayor's house. Someone phoned in a hot tip that he was running a bawdy house on the third floor." With that, Sterling hung up.

Judd gave a snort of laughter. Sterling could be counted on to keep a level head—although there had been moments when Judd had questioned his wisdom in getting involved with Jessica and her do-gooder deeds.

It had worked out for them. They were happy.

He swallowed against the knot that formed in his throat. No use pining for what used to be. He would ignore the clamoring in his blood. Soon Tracy would be gone, and his life would return to normal. It couldn't come too soon for him.

Tracy swept off the deck and dusted the patio furniture. She jumped and turned around when a young voice piped up from behind her.

"Hi." The neighbor boy bounced up the steps onto the deck.

"Hello," she said. "You must be Jimmy."

"Yeah. How did you know?"

"Judd said you were a friend."

Jimmy peered around her. "I came over to see his leg. Is it in a cast?"

"Yes. Come on. He's watching a ball game." She led the way into the family room where Judd sat with the TV on. She saw he'd changed from pajamas to a sport shirt and a pair of cutoffs.

"Hi, Sheriff." Jimmy went over to admire the injured leg, which was propped on a pillow on the coffee table. "Wow, did it hurt when you broke it? How did they get the cast on?"

Tracy smiled as she went to the kitchen. Maybe Judd's young friend would bring him out of his moody intro-spection. She'd certainly had no luck in cheering him up.

She poured two glasses of nonfat milk and arranged a variety of cookies on a plate. These she took to the family room and left for the patient and his guest to enjoy.

Grocery list in hand, she headed out, pausing to ask Jimmy to keep an eye on the sheriff.

"Sure," he said. "I can stay all afternoon. Mark has gone to visit his grandmother."

"Nice to know where I stand," Judd remarked.

Tracy laughed at his wry tone. "Number-two friend is pretty high on the totem pole, if you ask me."

His dark eyes roamed over her yellow slacks and bright-colored blouse. He opened his mouth, then closed it.

She was disappointed when he didn't speak. Scolding herself for wanting more than life offered, she hurried to the grocery store, then the bakery, then back to the house.

Jimmy was still there. He rose when she came into the house. "My mom called and said I had to come home when you got back. I'll come over tomorrow, if you like. I can bring a game to play. The sheriff likes checkers."

"That would be fine. Here, I bought too many of these apple turnovers. Maybe you and your mom would like some for dessert." She gave him a white bag.

"Thanks." He yelled a farewell to Judd, then bounded out of the house and across the yard. She saw him climb the rail fence.

She put the groceries away and straightened up the kitchen, then went into the family room. Judd was reading. The TV was on. The game was football instead of baseball. She smiled and settled in a chair with a magazine.

When she grew sleepy, she rested her head on the chair back and gazed at Judd. He'd gone to sleep.

His hair was thick, of a rich brown-black color. It waved smoothly back from his face. There was a suggestion of a widow's peak on his forehead.

She saw him draw a deep breath and exhale with a sighing sound. A storm grew in her, turbulent and demanding, until her body felt too small to hold it.

I love him, she thought, and knew the love had never gone away. It had lain dormant, like a seed in winter, waiting for the warmth of the sun to stir it to life. For her, Judd was that sun. She'd been back with him just a few days and her love had bloomed anew.

But what was she going to do with this love? It had no place in her future that she could see. Unless she could make Judd want her again...enough to ask her to stay.

She sniffed as tears pressed close to the surface. Judd opened his eyes and stared into hers. She knew the longing was there for him to see, and the love, if he cared to look.

The tears insisted on forming. She blinked them away as rapidly as she could.

"Don't," he said hoarsely.

"I'm all right. It's just..."

It was the hopelessness of the situation, of loving and not being able to do anything about it, but she couldn't say that. Her throat closed. She got to her feet, wanting to flee before she made a total fool of herself.

Judd stood, too. He took the three steps needed to bring him face-to-face with her. "Trace," he said and shook his head as if he, too, were in the grip of emotions too powerful to deny.

"I feel so lonely," she whispered.

He frowned as if in pain, then nodded slowly. "I know. God, I know." He reached out and touched her shoulder, then grasped her with both his hands. He drew her close.

She put her face into the groove of his neck and clasped her hands around his waist. For a while she was content to share the warmth of their embrace, then it wasn't enough.

Slowly, carefully, as if coaxing a wild creature, she ran her hands along his sides. Turning her head ever so little, she pressed her lips to the strong column of his neck.

She felt his breath catch. His hands tightened, then released her shoulders and slipped around her, pulling her against him.

"Trace," he said, a note of desperation in his voice.

"Hold me," she pleaded. "It's been so long."

He moved then, taking a seat on the sofa and pulling her across his lap. Her sandals hit the floor. His head bent, then his lips touched hers.

The kiss was so sweet it hurt.

She whimpered as the pent-up love crashed against the barrier of restraint she'd built inside. It had held too many years for her surrender to be an easy one. The ready tears burned her eyes as she fought for control.

"Oh, love, love," she murmured. She hadn't wanted to need to him like this, hadn't meant to let herself love him again.

The futility of fighting it swept over her. She couldn't give up the moment, no matter what tomorrow might bring.

"Make love to me." She remembered his leg. "Can we? Your leg ... does it hurt?"

"Shh, no, it doesn't hurt," he soothed, his lips busy at her eyes, her temples, her ears while his hands strayed all over her.

It felt so good to be touched and caressed. She loved the feel of him against her—big and strong and warm. With trembling hands, she unfastened his shirt.

"Take your blouse off," he requested in a low, husky tone that thrilled her with its urgency.

She stripped out of the bright silk print. Judd reached behind her and unfastened her bra with one hand. He hooked a finger at the front and pulled it from her. It whispered over her arms and disappeared behind her as he tossed it on the floor.

He brought her close, moving her from side to side so that her nipples brushed back and forth against the curly hairs on his chest. They beaded into hard, plump peaks at once.

Moving her so that she reclined against the arm of the sofa, he bent his head until he could reach one breast. He took the taut nipple into his mouth and ran his tongue around it, again and again. He remembered all the ways to drive her wild.

The sensuality that had always existed between them blossomed out of control. His hands touched her everywhere. When he unzipped her slacks, she twisted from side to side until he had them and the lacy underpants down her hips. They followed the rest of her clothing to the floor.

Against her hip, she felt the hard length of his phallus pulse against the denim of his cutoffs.

"The bedroom," he murmured. "I want to enjoy all of you without falling off the sofa."

When she opened her eyes, he smiled . . . so beautifully, it broke her heart. "I've missed that." She touched the corner of his mouth. "That slow, sexy smile…the way you look at a woman, as if she's the only one in your world…."

"You were. You were the only one," he avowed.

"But not anymore—"

He cut her off with his lips. When the kiss ended, he lifted her to her feet and pushed himself up from the sofa. He grabbed his crutches, hobbled a few steps, then paused and waited for her.

She stood there, rooted to the spot as love and fear collided inside her. She had no right to ask for anything from him—not his body, not his fidelity, not his love. But she wanted all of them.

"Are you coming?" he asked, a wariness in his manner.

He expected her to refuse, she realized. He thought she would turn from him as she'd done so long ago. He'd waited for her once, and she'd turned from him, lost in her own misery.

She took a step forward…then another. She felt she was on an ice bridge that might collapse beneath her at any moment.

When she came abreast of Judd, she walked past him and went to the master bedroom, feeling terribly exposed and vulnerable without her clothing. He fell into step behind her.

In the bedroom, she stopped beside the bed. She cast Judd an uncertain glance.

He bent and held the covers up with one hand, an invitation. She quickly climbed in. He propped the crutches against the wall.

Tracy watched as his hands went to the fastening of his cutoffs. He glanced at her, then turned his attention back to the task. His fingers trembled slightly as he worked the zipper.

Realizing he was as unsure of this moment as she was, she felt her own doubts ease up. They'd work it out, she decided. It would all work out.

"Hurry," she said. "I want you."

He pushed the cutoffs and briefs over his hips, then sat in the chair to work the clothing over the cast. When he rose and crossed the narrow space between the chair and bed, she laid her hand on his thigh, luxuriating in the feel of him.

"The first time I saw you, I thought you were a savage, wild and beautiful and free." She caressed his thigh, marveling at the hardness of the muscle beneath the taut skin.

When she touched him intimately, stroking the hard length of his erection, he made a low sound in the back of his throat, the sound of a man pushed beyond his limits.

With one mighty sweep, he threw the sheet aside. He pushed her down on the mattress and followed, dragging his injured leg up on the bed with a grunt of pain.

"Be careful," she said, worried that in their eagerness he might somehow injure it again.

"It's too late," he muttered hoarsely. He made a space for himself between her thighs. Then he pushed forward, his flesh hot and rigid against her as he sought entry.

She clasped his hips and drew him inside, pressing her hips upward to meet his downward thrust. Their bodies melded, sliding easily, snugly together. A perfect fit.

He took his weight on his elbows, his solid length covering her while he rested there. A shudder went through him.

"Don't move."

"I can't help it." She kissed his chest and nuzzled her nose through the crisp hairs. She flicked her tongue against his nipples and felt his body leap within her in response.

He tangled his fingers in her hair and angled her face up until her mouth was level with his. Then he kissed her. And kissed her. And kissed her.

It was wild and beautiful and desperate, each thrust of his tongue a sensuous prelude to the pleasure that would come later.

She clung to him helplessly, running her hands over his back and hips, along his thighs where the muscles were rigid with control. She vaguely realized she'd unleashed a tempest that wouldn't be contained until the final bolt of lightning jolted between them.

When he slipped a hand between them and stroked her lightly, an explosion of heat rippled through her. He rocked against her, then gasped and was still. She sensed he was fighting to hold back the climatic moment. There was no need.

She cried out as a great surge of tension coiled in her, then unfurled with the acute quickness of a whiplash.

Barriers fell by the wayside. Doubts were forgotten. There was only *now* and the pulsating intensity between them as he pounded into her, pushed over the edge by her climax.

Before she could think, the tension coiled again, then burst outward so that her entire body seemed to convulse around the point where he thrust so intimately, so pleasurably against her.

She clutched him desperately as the storm rode over her, blinding her, draining her. She heard him gasp, then his entire body went still. Inside, she felt the throbbing release of his seed. He started moving again, slower this time, until he at last rested, spent and panting, on her.

"So beautiful," she murmured, overcome by the intensity of their passion. "Oh, Judd, it was so beautiful." Tears slid down her temples into her hair.

Eleven

Judd thought beautiful didn't begin to describe what had happened between them. Mind-shattering, ecstatic... and, yeah, beautiful—all those terms applied, and then some.

He lingered, not wanting to break the connection between them, not wanting to think beyond the pure contentment of the moment.

And therein lay danger.

He'd been unable to deny the need between them, but he wouldn't become entangled with her again. He wouldn't let himself start thinking he had to have her in order to feel alive and whole, although that was the way he felt at the moment.

He'd been through that wringer once. When she'd told him she wanted a divorce, it had been like having open-heart surgery without benefit of anesthesia.

Her tears touched his cheek. He turned his head and sipped the salty moisture from her skin. Inside, something that had been hard and self-preserving went soft and mushy. He fought the need to comfort her.

Awkward with the cumbersome cast, he slowly eased away from her. The summer heat seeped into the house, but he felt the cold when he withdrew from the moist warmth of her body. He lay on his back and sighed as weariness riffled into every muscle.

He was aware of Tracy leaving the bed. He didn't open his eyes. He didn't want to see her go. She was a weakness he couldn't afford, he reminded himself. He had a job he liked in a town full of friends. He didn't need anything else.

A warm washcloth touched him in a sensitive place, causing him to jump in surprise. He heard her low murmur, reassuring him. Gently, she bathed him, then returned to the bathroom.

He lay there, feeling more vulnerable than he had at the moment of climax. A longing for the things they'd lost stalked his defenses. He felt exposed, his heart laid out raw and quivering on the primitive altar of...lust, he told himself, repeating the word until it felt hard and cold and pure in his mind.

Lust. That was all. Lust.

When Tracy returned to bed, she curled against him. She put one smooth thigh between his the way she used to and laid an arm over his chest. "Does this make your leg hurt?"

"No."

All pain had been burned away in the hot pounding of his blood through his body. He wiggled his toes, becoming aware of his injuries for the first time since he'd touched her. Caressing her hadn't bothered his sore hands at all.

Turning slightly, he eased an arm under her head and rested the other on her side. With his thumb, he began stroking the side of her breast. The slow buildup of heat started inside him. He wanted her again.

Ha, when had he ever stopped?

Even making love to another woman hadn't erased the memory of Tracy's response— He broke off the thought as another came to him. He hadn't offered her any protection.

Between them, it had never been necessary. Their clumsy eagerness had resulted in their son's conception almost as soon as they'd met. During the years after that, there'd been no need for birth control. Tracy had never conceived again.

He wondered if he should mention it. He owed it to her. He cleared his throat. "I didn't use a condom," he said.

She raised her head. Her eyes held that sleepy contentment he remembered so well. They also held a question.

"In case you were worried," he explained. "I'm safe. I've never been . . . you're the only woman I've ever had without taking the proper precautions."

He wasn't going to tell her there had been exactly two women in seven years, each of short duration as a lover. With Maris, he hadn't even gotten that far. He'd realized early on that they were destined to be only friends.

"I'm safe, too," Tracy said.

For a second, the idea of her with someone else burned a hole in him, then he thrust it aside. He thought he heard sadness in her softly spoken words, but couldn't figure it out.

"Was there someone?" he asked.

Tracy stiffened for a second, then sighed. Judd, once he was on to something, was more persistent than a hound after a rabbit.

"There was a man who wanted to marry me. I thought I loved him, too. In a way. Except that I couldn't . . . each time he touched me, I . . . froze."

That was when she'd gone to the psychologist, who'd told her it was time to get over her grief and on with her life. Tracy wondered what the woman would say now, if she talked about going to bed with Judd and about her wild response.

Was this going forward with her life, or backward?

"That didn't seem to be a problem this time." Judd stroked the side of her breast some more.

She detected a hint of satisfaction in the words. She frowned at him, letting her irritation show. "I suppose you never had any such problem with the women you've dated."

The slight smile disappeared from his mouth. "No," he said truthfully. "There weren't many."

She seethed with jealousy, knowing she had no right to, but feeling it just the same.

He touched the frown lines on her forehead. "Two. Very brief, very unsatisfactory."

A sigh of relief escaped her. She gave him a frank look. "I'm jealous, terribly jealous." She paused. "I saw Maris touch you the day I arrived and I wanted to hit her."

"Maris is a good friend, nothing more. It just wasn't there for us, for either of us. She met someone later."

"I know. Lily Mae told me she was married." Tracy sat up in bed and combed her tangled hair with her fingers. "Speaking of Lily Mae, she gave us some soup. Are you hungry?"

"Yes," he murmured, reaching over and clamping both hands around her waist. "For you." He sat her astride his hips. "You're going to have to do all the work this time."

She bent to him and planted a fierce kiss on his smiling mouth. "Gladly," she whispered, feeling the fire start all over again. It was a long time before she prepared their dinner.

After they ate, they sat on the sofa and watched TV or read. They ended up making love there, too. Neither of them could get enough of the other.

* * *

Tracy held the doors for Judd. When he was settled at his desk, she went into the conference room she used as an office and opened the FBI report. She read it through.

The expert at the forensic labs agreed with her analysis of the age of the bones. He'd also run a blood test. She looked at the type, then picked up the phone and dialed.

"Jackson, I have some news," she said when she reached the tribal attorney. "Kane sent me the report on the blood samples from the family who think the bones belong to their son. I got word on the bones from the FBI labs today. The chances of that being their long-lost boy are practically zilch. They have no common blood factors."

"They'll be disappointed. It's easier to accept death than to face the fact that the boy doesn't want to see them."

They chatted a few more minutes, then hung up. Tracy sat there lost in thoughts of the weekend. Yesterday, she and Judd had spent the entire day together. Their lovemaking had taken place at several spontaneous moments throughout the day, much as it had during their early marriage before Thadd's birth.

She smiled and yawned. Jimmy had come over after church and played checkers with Judd. Fortunately, about the time Judd had grown restless at the youngster's prolonged visit, Jimmy's friend Mark had returned home and come looking for him.

Tracy had sent the two boys off with a sack of cookies to tide them over until their dinner. Over the fence, she'd chatted with Jimmy's mother about a camping trip the boys would be taking in a couple of weeks with their scout troop, then she'd gone back inside.

Judd had been waiting impatiently for her. As soon as she was inside, he'd locked the front and back doors, closed the shutters and taken her to bed for a nap. Well, they had slept. Eventually.

Yawning again, she admitted she was happy. Beyond that, she wasn't going to think at present.

A knock at her door brought her to attention. "Come in."

Rafe Rawlings entered. "Hi. I have something for you." He handed her a package.

She opened it and found her knapsack and tools. Carefully, she and Rafe sifted through the broken glass of the sample bottles, but the evidence was gone. "Well, I'm pretty sure the short hairs belonged to our cowboy and the long one to...whoever."

"An Indian?" he asked. "A lot of them wear their hair like Jackson Hawk—long and tied in braids."

"No, it was probably a wo—" She stopped. That was evidence she meant only Judd and Jackson to have for now.

"A woman?" Rafe jumped right on the tidbit like a crow on a june bug. "Can you tell that by its size or something?"

"An expert doesn't have to explain her methods," Judd said from the open door. He limped inside, glad that he'd interrupted when he saw Tracy's smile of gratitude. "Sara Lewis called. She says she has Native American bones at the museum. Jackson thought you might be interested."

"Definitely." Tracy went to the cabinet. "I can compare the thigh bones to the one I have."

Judd observed the young policeman's interest as Tracy explained the bone characteristics of the three major human groups. When he left, Judd muttered, "I wonder what the hell he's up to?"

"I think he's looking for some clue to his parents," she said in a pensive tone. "It must be terrible to be totally abandoned by your family."

"Yeah." He eyed her as she prepared to leave. "Are you going to the museum?"

"Um-hmm."

"Don't go out to the site by yourself," he requested. He paused, then added, "I'm asking for your word on that."

She picked up the plastic bag with the femur tucked inside and went to him. "I promise," she murmured.

The scent of her cologne drifted around them. He remembered her splashing some at various places on her body after her shower that morning. The hunger rose in him.

Unable to resist, he caught her face between his hands and kissed her. A low growl of need escaped him. Every moment seemed to strengthen the bond between them.

When he let her up for air, they stared into each other's eyes, the passion plain to see. But there were other things there, too—the doubts and the questions.

Where was this going? When would it end?

The telephone on Tracy's desk rang. She reached out and flicked on the speaker, her eyes still dazed from their embrace. A sense of pride pushed its way into his consciousness. At least he did the same thing to her that she did to him.

He limped back to his office and sat down. Propping his foot on the desk, he picked up a report. But his mind stayed on Tracy.

She was talking to the FBI office, telling them what was going on with the case. "This week?" he heard her say.

His attention caught, he listened as she told her boss that she was sure they'd find more evidence soon. The man was against spending any more time on it.

"Okay, the end of the week," Tracy said. "Yes, I'll be off the case then. I'll tell the sheriff."

Judd realized he didn't want to know. Darkness hovered near, threatening to descend at any moment. When she told him she was leaving, what would he say?

Hell, he'd probably break into tears and beg her to stay. She had to know he wanted her. He'd accepted her into his house and his bed. Didn't that tell her how he felt?

He ran a hand over his face and searched for the emptiness that had saved him before. It wasn't there. She'd slipped in and filled every lonely crevice of his life. When she left . . .

Tracy finished her call. She walked into his office with her purse and bag in her hands. He noticed she didn't meet his eyes. Instead, she'd gone quiet . . . the way she had before she'd finally admitted the end of their marriage.

To his surprise, she knelt beside him and wrapped her arms around his neck. She kissed him. It felt like goodbye.

The secretary stuck her head in the outer door. "Hey, Boss, Sterling wanted to— Oh, excuse me."

Tracy let him go and stood. A flush crept into her cheeks. The secretary grinned.

"What was Sterling's problem?" Judd managed to ask in a level voice.

"He wanted to let you know the raid on the mayor's house went fine. They arrested this little old gray-headed woman who insisted she was the mayor's mother . . . as if we were stupid hick cops who'd believe that."

Tracy's mouth dropped open.

Judd closed it gently with a fist under her chin. "A hick cop's idea of a joke," he explained, a smile lighting his face. "Tell Sterling to use the rubber hoses on the little old lady. We're after a full confession."

* * *

Tracy was still grinning when she left, after promising Judd she'd be back promptly at noon. A short time later she pulled into the parking lot of the Native American museum.

Several other cars were there. She noticed the license plates. Lots of tourists on the road in August, apparently.

Sara Lewis was busy with a scout troop, but she stopped long enough to show Tracy where the bones were kept.

Tracy was impressed. The collection was housed in protective drawers the same as the Smithsonian used for their archives.

An hour of comparing thigh bones assured her she was right. Her bones belonged to an Anglo, a white cowboy who had trusted the other person enough to turn his back on him...or her, she mused, thinking of the long blond hair with the dark root.

The two-faced woman?

Tracy pictured the setting as she closed the last drawer and repacked her bone. A clandestine meeting...a lover's quarrel...anger...a thrown rock...then...

But women rarely displayed the type of fury that would result in bashing a person in the back of the head, even if they had knocked the victim down with a rock thrown in anger. Maybe some jealous husband had bashed the cowboy after seeing the young man with his wife. That was more likely.

Anyway, it was all speculation. A scientist was supposed to present the evidence, not make up wild stories.

"Did our collection help?" Sara asked when Tracy emerged from the back room.

"Yes. Thanks so much for letting me use it." She told the young curator what she'd found and headed back to the office. She needed to call Jackson and tell him the news so that the tribe could quit worrying about the bones. And the case. It was out of their hands.

In fact, it was now in Judd's jurisdiction. He'd be glad of that. She'd tell him over lunch. Maybe they would have a quiet meal together while they went over the case. Alone in the office while the secretary was at lunch. She smiled.

When she entered Judd's office half an hour later, she stopped abruptly. A woman was there with him. Holding his hand.

"You poor dear," the Kincaid woman was saying. "When I heard the news, I couldn't believe someone had tried to hurt you. This is all so strange. I thought small towns were supposed to be safe from all that."

"I guess people are the same the world over," Judd remarked.

Rather facetiously, Tracy thought. She noticed he wasn't trying to get his hand loose from the treacly female, whose name she couldn't recall. But she was married to Dugin Kincaid.

"Hello, Mrs. Kincaid," Tracy said brightly, bustling in and breezing toward her own office. She noticed the china plates, the silverwear and napkins on Judd's desk, all showing signs of a recent meal. She did a slow boil. "You brought lunch. How nice."

"The cook out at the ranch knows how much I like Cornish pies," Judd hurriedly said. "Mary Jo brought two in. I insisted she eat with me. We talked about the case."

"It's so interesting. I'd no idea a forensic detective could tell so much just by digging around and looking at old bones." Mary Jo gave her a gentle smile. "The news report said it was a cowboy. However could you tell that?"

Tracy felt like a heel. The woman was extremely nice. "By the shape of the pubic bone," she said.

"Oh," Mary Jo said. She actually blushed. "Oh, I see."

Judd covered a grin as Tracy stared in astonishment. She hadn't known anyone was that inhibited in this day and age.

"Well," Mary Jo said, getting to her feet. "I suppose I'd better go. I have some errands to run."

Tracy murmured a farewell and closed the door to her room. She replaced her evidence and went over all the reports, including her own, to make sure she hadn't missed anything.

Judd came in a few minutes later. He propped himself on the corner of the table. "Did you have lunch?"

She shook her head.

"I assumed you would eat before you came back. That's why I invited Mary Jo to share the lunch with me."

"And she was so interested in the case, especially your injuries, I noticed," Tracy replied sweetly.

"Jealous, Trace?"

She took a deep breath, aware of his dark gaze on her every second. "Yes," she admitted.

"Then you know how I feel about your old friend Jackson Hawk and your new friend Rafe Rawlings."

"Yes, I understand." She faced him. "Judd, where do we go from here?" It was an issue she didn't want to discuss, but she had to know.

"I wish the hell I knew." He lifted her hand and clasped it between his palm and his thigh. "I only know I don't want you to leave. I can't give you up, not yet."

To her, that implied he could give her up when he'd gotten his fill of her. She wondered how long that would take.

Tracy stretched her weary back. She and Rafe Rawlings, who'd volunteered to help her on his day off, had searched the area along the base of the cliff for hours.

She'd spent the rest of the week combing the narrow bank in hopes of finding something.

Disgruntled, she sat on a boulder and ate an apple while staring at the creek. The water was at its lowest level now, but in spring, with snowmelt from the mountains, it turned into a dangerous torrent. No telling where or how far debris might be carried in the rushing current.

"Giving up?" Rafe asked.

She nodded. "This could take years."

He hobbled over, then plopped down beside her. He looked at the river. "Yeah."

"Yet I have this feeling...." She shook her head. She knew there were more clues, if only she could find them. She sighed, then laughed. "I'm like a prospector. I'm sure I'm going to find gold around the next bend."

"Why don't you ask Winona for help?"

"In case she can see where the other bones are?"

"Yeah. Why not?" he asked at her surprised glance. "What do you have to lose?"

"You're right." She jumped to her feet. "I'll take a bone to her." She laughed at how that sounded.

"Come in, you two," Winona called from the door.

"Help me watch for those damned goats," Judd told Tracy.

She handed him the crutches after he'd maneuvered himself out of her compact car. Reaching in the back seat, she withdrew the bag with the pelvis inside, having decided that it was the most likely bone to invoke a sense of who the person had been.

"How's the missing-persons search going?" Winona asked, holding the door open so Judd could get inside.

"Well, we have a few possibilities. Judd has been checking the state and FBI lists through the computer for me this week." Tracy took the crutches and set them out of the way when Judd was seated. She pulled the footstool over and propped his leg up. "Is that comfortable?"

"Yes," he said grumpily. "You don't have to wait on me hand and foot. I'm fine."

"He's been on his feet way too much this week. Kane saw us at the café last night. He checked Judd's leg and told him to stay off it and keep it propped up until the swelling has gone down," she explained to Winona, ignoring his scowl as she put a pillow under the cast.

Winona sided with Tracy. "You should take care of yourself," she told Judd. "You'll end up with arthritis in that leg, then you'll be sorry."

"Is that a prediction?" he snapped. "I'm sorry," he went on before she could speak. "I'm in a hell of a mood."

"If you'd take the painkillers Kane gave you, you might feel better," Tracy put in with no sympathy.

"All right. Give me two. And don't complain when I fall asleep in the middle of dinner."

"We wouldn't think of it," Tracy told him coolly. "Winona, I brought the pelvis with me. Do you feel up to doing anything with it, or would you rather wait until after we eat?"

"Let's do it now."

Tracy nodded. She removed the evidence from the bag and carried it to the psychic.

"What do you want to know?" Winona asked, laying it in her lap and placing both hands on the bony structure.

"Who it belongs to?" Judd said dryly.

Tracy gave him a be-quiet-and-don't-be-so-cynical look. "Or where the skull is," she added. "That would help a lot."

Winona closed her eyes. Tracy pulled a chair close and sat down quietly. They waited.

A minute went by. Another. Five minutes. Six.

Winona opened her eyes. "Nothing is coming to me, except a few vague images. I can't force it," she apologized.

"I know." Tracy patted her arm.

Winona gasped and pulled away.

Tracy shot a questioning look at her, but the older woman's eyes were closed. "Tell me what you see, no matter how odd," she requested, bending close but not touching.

"A child, alone and frightened, crying...dark... woods all around...he's lost...falling...falling... you must save him...."

Tracy was disappointed. She knew the vibes Winona was picking up came from Rafe Rawlings. His personal quest to find his parents was messing up her quest to find the rest of the bones, darn it.

She laid a hand on Winona's shoulder. "It's okay. You can let it go."

Winona moved away as if stung. Tracy hesitated, not sure what to do. She'd never seen her friend so pale.

"Leave her alone," Judd said quietly. "What do you see?" he asked the psychic.

"The woman, the two-faced woman. Two men, fighting." She shook her head. "Too many images...too hard to see...a child is crying...Tracy...crying...help her, Judd, help Tracy."

Tracy looked at Judd, but his attention was glued on Winona. She swallowed against the knot of emotion that had formed at the mention of a child. Her own memories must have interfered with the reading, even though she'd made her peace with the past. Or perhaps it was the future Winona was seeing.

Winona opened her eyes. She handed the pelvis back to Tracy. "I'll try and describe the images I saw as they came to me. First, I saw two men fighting, then they disappeared. Next there was a child lost in the woods. That was after you touched me. It wasn't Thadd," she quickly stated.

Tracy looked up to find Judd watching her with concern. The longing that had grown all week surfaced. She wanted another child with him. She wanted him to ask her to stay and make a new life. She wanted him to tell her how very much he loved her.

But he hadn't, and she couldn't ask.

"It was Rafe Rawlings," Tracy explained. "He worked with me at the site today. He was probably the child you saw lost in the woods. That was where he was found, remember?"

Winona nodded. "But then the first image came back—the two men fighting. One of them was the person whose bones you found. I'm sure of that. The two-faced woman was there. But then the scene shifted and I saw you and Judd and many others." She frowned as she studied Tracy. "You were worried about someone. That was all. I don't know if any of the images were connected. They could have been entirely random events."

"Yes," Judd said sardonically. "There seems to be a lot of skeletons in a lot of closets in the county."

Tracy fetched him water and two tablets. "Let me help you with supper," she suggested to Winona.

It was time for a lighter mood. Judd was obviously tired and in pain. She didn't feel good either, in spite of a week of ecstasy in Judd's arms. It was only while they were making love that she could forget the distance between them. At those moments, they were of one mind, one body... but not one heart.

Judd was keeping his under lock and key.

"Is it that bad?" Winona asked softly when they were in the tiny kitchen.

Tracy glanced over her shoulder. Judd was catching the evening news on TV. He couldn't hear them. "What do you mean?"

"You sighed as if life were a burden you'd as soon put down." Winona checked the vegetable stew in the Crockpot. "From what I've heard, things are pretty cozy between the sheriff and the FBI lady these days."

"Lily Mae, no doubt," Tracy said with a wry smile.

"And others. Don't give up on him. You two shared something precious once. You can have it again. If you're not afraid to ask for it."

"He hasn't asked me to stay."

Winona gave an impatient snort. "Have you told him you want to? He's not a mind reader, you know." She grinned. "In fact, he's damned obtuse, if you ask me. He's waiting for you to make the first move."

"Do you think so?" Tracy wanted to believe her mentor, but uncertainty rose, jarring her confidence.

The rest of the evening passed in a pleasant blend of food and conversation. They sat outside while the sky changed from twilight to dark. At ten, Tracy herded Judd into the car.

Winona gave her a meaningful stare before they drove off.

The dark interior of the car held a quiet, intimate ambiance that Tracy didn't want to break. She'd wait until they arrived at the house before she said anything, she decided.

Fear ate at her. The seventeen-mile trip had never seemed shorter. Once home, she fussed over Judd, getting him inside and settled on the family-room sofa, then dashing off to bring him a glass of water and two of his pills. She knew he was hurting. He looked very grim and tense around the eyes.

"Will you stop fluttering around?" he finally snapped. "You may as well tell me what's on your mind."

She sat in an easy chair. The time had come to ask what his intentions were for their future.

What if he didn't want her to stay?

Twelve

"I talked to my boss on this project Monday afternoon," Tracy began tentatively. "As of now, I'm off the case. We agreed, if I didn't find anything else this week, to call it quits. As far as the federal government is concerned, it's your bailiwick now."

"Yeah, I heard the conversation." His face held no expression that she could detect. He kept his gaze focused on the TV, which he'd turned to a news channel, but with the sound off.

"The tough lawman who doesn't let emotion cloud his life," she muttered, feeling it was useless to talk to him. She'd felt that way before. She closed her eyes and pressed her thumb and finger against her forehead, where a faint headache nagged.

"What the hell does that mean?"

"It means I can walk out of here tomorrow and never darken your door again ... if that's what you want." She tried to smile, but her mouth wobbled.

The silence trembled between them. She recalled Winona's advice about speaking her mind and heart.

"Or I can stay ... longer," she added, unable to ask for a lifetime. "I have some time before I report to a dig."

"A dig?" He glanced at her, then away.

"A Smithsonian fellowship to examine a find in South America. The bones may be Spanish. If so, the Conquistadors penetrated farther south during that era than previously thought.''

''I see.'' His wariness was a barrier between them. Perhaps the chasm of distrust was too wide to ever be breached.

She hoped not. She was filled with so many wants. She wanted his love, his faith in their future. She wanted him to love her, to believe in her and her love. They'd had all that at one time, but somehow it had been lost, tragedy added to tragedy.

She knew now she wanted to go forward. She wanted a new life . . . with this man.

''Once,'' she said, ''we needed each other, but we failed, both of us. You walked out when I needed you. I did the same to you.'' She stopped as sadness threatened to overtake her. ''You told me, that day I went to the cemetery, that you were sorry. I'm sorry, too, for turning away when you came to me.''

He closed his eyes. His face wore a stricken expression. ''It doesn't matter now.''

''It does to me.'' She gathered her courage. ''I want to stay, at least for a while longer. Once we had something special. I'd like to find it again. If you want the same thing, then you must tell me,'' she said in a strained voice. She couldn't keep the tremor out of it. She stared at the man on TV, his mouth moving but no words coming out.

''What if we don't find it?'' Judd asked. ''Then what?''

''I don't know,'' she said truthfully.

She held the despair at bay. Somewhere in her heart, she believed he loved her, but the years of separation would take time to heal. If he never trusted her enough to let that love show, then she would have to accept that.

Uncertain and afraid, she nevertheless went to him, taking a seat beside him on the sofa. She needed the comfort of his nearness. He put an arm around her and held her close.

"Stay," he finally said. "We'll take each day as it comes."

"Yes." She'd have to accept that . . . for now.

Tracy walked along the bluff. Behind her, Rafe paused and inspected the spot where Judd had gone over the ledge. She stopped and waited for him. After wiping her face with a handkerchief, she took a long drink from her canteen.

"Who else has been up here?" Rafe asked.

"Sterling helped me find Judd."

"Um, this must be his print then."

"It couldn't be. It's rained since then."

"Then someone else has been scouting around. Here's where he stopped and looked at the place where the rock broke off."

She went over and examined the area, dropping to her haunches beside the young cop. When he pointed, she saw the prints, side by side, the boot heels digging deeper into the thin dirt beside the rocky outcropping.

"Whoever it was, he was sitting here just like we are, checking the evidence."

Goose bumps ran up her neck. She glanced behind them uneasily. It was unnerving that a killer might be on the loose and watching everything they did. He had already tried to put Judd out of the way.

Briefly, Tracy wondered if the wolf monster had thought the sheriff was more of a threat than she, the forensic expert. Or was the person merely in a panic and trying to scare everyone away from the spot?

She studied the land. There was more evidence to be found. She could feel it in her bones. She had to smile at her own play on words.

"I want to check around at the limestone knob. Somehow I think we're overlooking something."

"Right."

Rafe gave her a hand up, and they trudged along the steep slope to the "egg rock", as she'd dubbed it to herself. She knelt and peered under the jutting edge of the overhang. It formed a cozy little cave. High enough to sit in. For a short person. Such as a kid.

"Um," she said.

"What?"

"This would make a neat cave for a kid to play in. As an adult, they'd remember it."

Rafe nodded. "I follow you. Someone who found the cave when they lived in the area as a kid might come back to it if they needed a place to hide something."

"Right. Let's do some more digging." She took her rock pick and began testing the floor of the shallow cavern. To one side, where the crack in the overhead limestone admitted water, she found dirt. She realized that erosion had formed a runoff channel, which had filled with dirt and debris over time. She began excavating.

"Let me," Rafe requested when she grew tired. He took over the job of breaking the hard soil and moving it out from under the rocky overhang. She sifted through it, but found nothing.

"Be easy," she said. "If there is bone, I don't want to shatter it."

"No problem." He handled the pick almost tenderly.

Two hours later they took a break.

"So, looks like things are back on for you and the sheriff?" Rafe asked as they each drank a cold soda from a cooler he'd toted up from his truck.

She smiled. That was the question on everyone's mind, it seemed. The townsfolk weren't hesitant about voicing it, either. Lily Mae had announced the news for all and sundry at the Hip Hop Café when Tracy and Judd had joined the widow for dinner two nights ago.

"For now," she admitted.

"And tomorrow?" he asked softly.

She managed a smile. "Who knows what tomorrow will bring?"

"Yeah." He stared out at the lush valley, lost in his own thoughts, which Tracy thought were sad.

Before she had time to reflect on the man who'd been abandoned in the woods by his family, she detected a movement at the far edge of her vision. Every nerve in her body sprang to instant alert.

Without speaking, she reached over and touched Rafe's arm, then let her hand drop to the rock pick beside her.

He glanced at her in question. Seeing the warning on her face, he, too, became alert to possible danger. "Where?" he asked in a low, conversational tone.

She cut her eyes to where she'd seen the shadowy form behind a thicket of pine and chaparral. Picking up her cola, she drank from the can and let her gaze roam the woods to her left. She realized she and Rafe were totally exposed on the rocky knob.

A face appeared above the tangled brush under the trees. The man had tanned, leathery skin, with a hatchet of a nose, the bluest eyes she'd ever seen and the wildest hair—half gray, half russet, the shade of rusted metal. He looked like a madman.

She gasped.

Rafe whipped a glance at her, then in the direction she was staring. "Oh," he said. A smile turned the corners of his mouth upward. "Homer, come on out," he called.

The man emerged from the thicket, his manner suspicious of them, as if he considered them interlopers on his terrain.

His clothing was old. It fit loosely on his bony frame. Tracy had the impression of a man who was slowly fading away, until nothing would be left but a lonely spirit. It was an odd thought.

"Hey, Homer, I'm Rafe Rawlings. You remember me? We met when you were prospecting over on our ranch a few years ago."

The old man drew himself up with a show of dignity. "Of course I remember. I'm not daft." He grinned unexpectedly. His teeth were surprisingly white and even. "Although lots of folks would like to think that."

"This is Tracy. . ." Rafe paused and looked at her.

"Roper," she said. "Tracy Roper." She remembered him vaguely. She and her father had run across him in the woods a few times while they were looking for artifacts.

Homer nodded. "I knew your father. He still teaching?"

"Yes. What are you prospecting for—gold?" she asked.

His face immediately took on a secretive, wary expression. "Maybe, maybe not," was his response. He obviously didn't like the question and was suspicious of the person who asked it.

"Or sapphires," Rafe suggested. "There used to be a mine in these parts, but the stones weren't gem quality. Homer, were those your boot prints I saw over by the bluff where Judd went off?"

"I was just looking," the man said at once. "I didn't do it."

"I know. I just wondered—did you happen to be up here when that happened?"

Homer glanced around the woods, but didn't answer.

"Did you see anyone?" Tracy asked.

The old mountain man shook his head in denial. "It wasn't a person," he said in a near whisper. "It was...something else."

"What?" Rafe asked, his tone a little harder.

"One of the spirits," Homer informed them. "They don't like people in their territory."

"Is this their territory?"

Homer quickly scanned the area. "You know it is. It's sacred ground. You shouldn't be here. Sometimes I can calm them down, but not always."

Tracy wondered how long the old man had roamed the woods. He looked ancient, but age was hard to tell on a person who had spent a great deal of time outdoors. Exposure to the elements aged one excessively.

"You couldn't calm this one?" Rafe persisted.

"No." Homer came closer. He seemed worried. "It was a different one. I'd never seen it before."

She noticed his boots were new and wondered if someone had bought them for him. Indians had a special respect for eccentrics and such. Perhaps some of them watched out for the old prospector.

"You two had better be careful," he advised. He turned and walked back into the woods, disappearing into the trees.

"An oddball, but harmless," Rafe said.

Tracy hefted the rock pick. "Well, back to work." She didn't have much hope of finding anything. Her confidence in the project had evaporated. "This is the last day I spend on the case," she said.

"Hmm." Rafe clearly didn't believe her. "You're as dedicated to finding your artifacts, as you call 'em, as Homer is to finding that old sapphire mine."

"Nope, this is it. I've had it." She knelt and slammed the pick into the rocky crevice just beyond the rock overhang. When she pulled it free, a chunk of stone slid aside, revealing an eroded area underneath. Mostly out of idle curiosity, she dug the dirt out of the groove in the limestone.

The pick hit another object. Careful now, she scraped the dirt and leaf mold away. A white, rounded object became visible.

"I'll be damned," Rafe muttered beside her. He began working with her, removing the soil with his hands as she loosened it.

The object soon became visible. It was a skull.

They worked slowly, freeing the bone from the soil packed around and in it. When Tracy lifted it from its bed, it came out intact. She turned it over.

Chill bumps raced along her scalp.

The back of the skull showed a pattern of distinct fractures that radiated outward like a starburst. A few chips of bone were missing. "Here's where he was hit." She showed Rafe.

After emptying the dirt from the brain pan, she put the skull in a bag, then sifted through the soil. She found some short hairs similar to those she'd found before. That was it.

A crack of thunder had them scurrying to finish. "That's it," she said after they'd dug out the entire runoff channel.

They left at a trot, hurrying to beat the rain they could see in the distance like gray curtains obscuring the hills. At Rafe's truck, Tracy jumped in and laid her new knapsack—a gift from Judd—on the floor. She kept the bone bag in her lap.

In town, Rafe let her out at the police station. She dashed inside with her treasures, feeling much like she thought the old hermit might feel if he found his mine—buoyant of spirit and full of excitement.

The case was all but solved. The skull had a full set of teeth still attached. Now it was a matter of matching them.

She was assuming the cowboy was a local man, not a drifter who'd been passing through, and therefore had dental records in town. Another conclusion based on gut feelings rather than evidence, she acknowledged.

Judd wasn't in when she arrived. The secretary said he was out on a case with Sterling. A child was missing.

"A child? Who?"

"The little boy who lives next door to Judd."

"Jimmy? He was on a camping trip with his scout troop," Tracy said, recalling the fact. "He and his friend, Mark." A terrible fear seized her heart and wouldn't let go. It was the way she'd felt when they'd searched for Thadd those many years ago.

"Are you all right?" The secretary stepped closer.

Tracy nodded. "Yes. I need to call Winona." She went around Judd's desk, set the bone bag and knapsack on the corner and picked up the telephone. "Winona, have you heard about Jimmy?" she asked as soon as the woman answered. The secretary left the room.

"Yes. There was a news flash on the radio a moment ago."

"Can you come?" Tracy asked.

"Of course."

"Meet me at the house . . . Judd's place," she clarified. "The soccer ball is there. Maybe you can pick up something from it."

"There's no need. I already am," the psychic said.

Tracy realized Winona was getting something now. She waited, hardly breathing, until the vision was over.

"Yes, a hole, darkness," Winona said. "A mine... air...yes, the air shaft...wait, something else...the woman...the two-faced woman..." She was silent, then said, "It's hopeless. It's all mixed up. I can't sort through the images."

Tracy sighed in disappointment. Fear gnawed at her. Jimmy, with his sunny disposition, had entertained Judd so sweetly. The world would be a lesser place if he died.

As if echoing her worries, the thunder rumbled again. "Oh, no, the rain," she muttered. She said goodbye and ran to the outer office. "Where is Judd? I've got to go to him."

"He's out at the Kincaid spread. Here, I'll show you." The secretary got out a map. "That's where the kids are camping, near the spring that feeds the stock pond in this section. Take the mountain pass, then turn right at the old Baxter ranch. There's a sign."

"Thanks." Tracy rushed to her car and took off. She wanted to be with Judd. If Jimmy wasn't found—she wouldn't allow herself to think of him as dead—then Judd would need her. He'd feel responsible for finding the boy and seeing that he was safe.

It seemed hours, but finally she arrived at the Baxter ranch road. Several cars were already there, so it was no problem finding the spot. She found Judd and Sterling sectioning off a map for the search routine.

Mary Jo Kincaid was pouring coffee, made on a portable burner. She had boxes of cookies and doughnuts on a camping table beside the huge coffeepot. Two scoutmasters stood close by, wearing identical worried expressions. Dugin Kincaid was there, too, looking rather at a loss.

Tracy spoke to Mary Jo, accepted a cup of coffee and went to stand by Judd. He didn't speak, but rested a hand at the back of her waist while he finished giving orders for the search.

In ten minutes the search parties left, each squad commander carrying a walkie-talkie. Judd stayed by the radio to take their calls and give further orders. While the search was on, parents arrived to collect their sons and were asked to return home rather than stay and clog the access road.

As night and the storm drew closer, the desperation of the search-and-rescue team became quietly dogged. A horse-and-dog patrol scouted the ravines at the base of the mountains, while the other searchers formed a phalanx that moved steadily through the woods, each person in sight of the next so that no bit of ground was overlooked.

When night came, the workers were called in. It would be too easy to miss an unconscious child in the dark. Tracy prayed that the storm would hold off. So far, it had.

She milled around while Judd gave orders for the next day's search, which would begin at first light. He unrolled two sleeping bags in the back of the truck. He and Tracy slept there that night, curled together against the cold.

Lily Mae came out with bacon and eggs and biscuits the next morning. "You're a godsend," Judd told her.

"Nothing keeps the spirits up like hot food," the widow said, not missing a beat in her self-appointed duties. She handed him and Tracy steaming cups of coffee to go with their meal, then went to Jimmy's mother and forced her to eat. She looked as if she were staring death in the face. The Kincaids arrived with more coffee and doughnuts.

The search continued.

Tracy was more and more concerned about Judd. His face held a pasty grayness under his tan. His eyes were haunted by memories neither of them could keep at bay. They'd been through this eight years ago, and the pain was just as sharp now.

Sometimes she felt like railing at an indifferent God who would let a child be hurt; at other times she prayed feverishly. Mostly she sat by Jimmy's mother, quietly staying close.

"How did you stand it?" the woman asked at one point. "When it was your child . . . how could you bear it?"

"You just do. It's hard, but you do. Don't give up hope. It's early yet." Tracy looked at the leaden sky and prayed hard that the rain would hold off another day.

They waited at the camping site, listening to the reports of sectors being covered by the searchers. It was noon on Saturday when they got word.

"He's here! He's alive!" a sector boss yelled from the radio.

Jimmy's mother put her hands to her face.

Judd listened to the report. "Okay," he said. "We'll move down there to plan the operation." He signed off and spoke to the waiting group. "Jimmy fell into an air shaft of an old mine while he was out exploring. One of the dogs took a point on it. The boy answered when the men called down the shaft. Now we have to get him out. Let's go."

They packed up and headed for the new site. The old mine was in one of the ravines, a rough area of steep-walled minicanyons and loose, rocky soil. Tracy felt her heart sink as she thought of cave-ins and various other dangers.

A mining expert was brought in by helicopter. "Too dangerous," he said in answer to a question on digging out the collapsed tunnel from the abandoned mine. "The ground is unreliable. The best bet is to have someone go down the shaft, tie a rope around the kid and haul him out.''

''How?'' One of the Boy Scout leaders asked.

''The person would have to be lowered headfirst into the hole.'' The engineer measured the width of the shaft.

Someone gasped. Tracy glanced up, to see Lily Mae clamping a hand over her mouth. The widow's first husband had been caught in a rock slide. His horse had lost its footing and fallen over, crushing the man as they slid down the mountain in a tumble of rocks.

''It would have to be someone small,'' the engineer continued, studying the diameter of the hole, ''someone who can think in a dangerous situation.''

''I'll go,'' Judd said.

Tracy gaped at him. ''You can't,'' she said.

''I will,'' said the Scout leader, an older man with gray hair and a paunch.

The engineer shook his head, clearly considering the man unsuitable for the job.

''Make a rope harness,'' Judd told Sterling. ''I'll need one for the kid, too.''

''Don't be ridiculous.'' Tracy grabbed his arm. ''You have a broken leg.''

''I used to do some spelunking when I was younger,'' Sterling said, stepping up to volunteer.

''Both of you are too big. Your shoulders won't fit,'' the expert stated, dismissing them.

''I'll go,'' Tracy said. ''I'm an anthropologist. I've been in some tight places digging out artifacts.''

The engineer looked her over and nodded. ''You'll do.''

''No.'' Judd stepped between Tracy and the man. ''Not her.''

''She's our best bet. We'd have to shore up the ground every step of the way if we try digging the boy out.''

"We can widen the air shaft," Judd decided. He looked at Sterling. "It would be dangerous."

Sterling didn't hesitate. "I can handle it."

"No!" Tracy exclaimed, anger forming a tight ball inside her. "The hole might cave in if you try to enlarge it. I'll go."

"Like hell," Judd said, flatly refusing.

She turned on him. "There's a child down there," she said in a quieter voice.

They stared eye-to-eye, neither blinking. Everyone watched the drama as if momentarily turned to statues.

"A child," she repeated in a low, intense tone.

At last he nodded. "You'll do exactly as you're instructed. If it starts to go, we'll yank you out. Don't fight me on this," he warned when she opened her mouth to argue. "Sterling," he snapped. "You'll handle the operation."

"I want you to," Tracy said stubbornly.

Judd looked at the clouds, then nodded grimly.

She turned to the engineer. "What should I watch out for?"

While he explained the composition of the loosely packed soil, Judd and Sterling planned the descent. Sterling made a harness from climbing ropes for her and another for Jimmy. All she had to do was snap it around the boy's waist and over his chest.

Judd buckled her into the climbing rig. He limped over to the mouth of the air shaft, where the mother talked soothingly to her son. He could hear Jimmy crying down below.

"Tracy is coming to get you," his mother said.

"Hey, Jimmy," Judd called. "It's the sheriff. I need to know something. Is your head up or down?"

"Down, sort of," he answered. "It's wider at the bottom. I'm sideways, sort of scrunched up."

"Can you tell if anything is broken?"

"Maybe my arm. It hurts something awful." He started sobbing again. "I want out. I want to go home."

"Right. Here comes Tracy. She'll get you."

Taking the rope for Jimmy in one hand, she indicated she was ready. The engineer adjusted the angle of the mining light on her head. She lay down on a tarp placed at the edge of the shaft and started wiggling her way inside.

Two strong hands caught her legs and lifted them into the air, hooking her toes into loops in the rope. "There," Sterling said. "That should help."

"Jerk on the rope when you're ready to come up," Judd told her. "Or if there's trouble."

She looked at him, her heart in her eyes. *I love you,* she silently told him. He gave her a harsh glance, then bent over the winch, checking the brake device. She pulled her arms in to her body and nodded for them to start.

It did give her a more secure feeling to have her feet anchored to something, even if it was the rope, which felt rather flimsy all of a sudden. Judd started cranking the winch that let her down into the blackness of the earth. Sterling guided her until he had to let go.

She was on her own.

Judd watched Tracy's feet disappear into the maw of the hole. He fought an urge to reverse the winch and bring her back to safety. A hand closed on his shoulder.

"Let me take over here," Sterling suggested. "You stay by the hole and keep a hand on the ropes. That way, you can tell if something is happening."

Judd nodded. He let his chief detective take the winch. He moved over to the hole and sat on the tarp, placed there to keep the loose soil from being dislodged into the hole. He put his hands on the two ropes and at once felt connected to Tracy.

This was their best bet for saving the boy, but it also put her in danger so real it was like a metallic taste in his mouth. Fear for her stuck in the back of his throat.

If she died . . .

God, he couldn't think about it—not now, when her life hung by this rope slipping steadily through his hands. He had to force himself not to close his fist and stop that downward drop. If anything happened to her . . .

He forced himself to finish the thought. If anything happened to her, then it would be over for him, too. It was that simple.

"Slow down," he said.

Sterling reeled out the rope at a slow, steady pace. Judd suppressed the need to yell down to Tracy and ask if she was okay.

"I'm almost there," she called out. "Slow. Slower," she directed. Her voice seemed miles away rather than fifty feet down.

He tested the tension on the line. She wasn't at the bottom.

"I see him," she cried, excitement in her voice. "Stop."

"Stop," he said to Sterling, although the detective had already stopped cranking. They could hear Tracy clearly.

From one side, he heard Jimmy's mother sobbing.

"A bit more," Tracy directed. "Let me down another foot. Do it slowly."

They fed the line out inch by inch.

"Hold," she called up.

Judd heard a different note in her voice. Something was wrong. He bent closer over the hole. His heart stopped. From far below, he could hear the tinkling sound of falling rock . . . a trickle of sound that sent a chill of fear into his soul.

"The ground is starting to go," he said tersely. "Get ready to haul her out of there." He called softly down the shaft. "Get ready, Trace. We're bringing you up."

She didn't answer.

"Trace?" he called again. The sounds from below grew more ominous. "Get her out of there," he ordered.

"No, wait," Tracy protested. "Judd, not yet . . . I'm almost . . ."

They heard a deep, low rumble, then a shock wave shook the ground under them.

"Jimmy!" his mother cried. "Oh, my God, *Jimmy.*"

"Pull," Judd shouted at Sterling. He moved to the winch and put his hands beside the deputy's. Together they worked furiously, winching the rope out of the hole as dirt caved in on the shaft that had provided fresh air to the mine long ago.

The earth around the mouth of the hole started falling in, tiny landslides that sounded as loud as thunder in the hearts of the people who watched.

No one spoke.

Another quake rumbled under their feet. Jimmy's mother cried out once more and buried her face against the Scout master. Tears streamed down his own face as he silently watched.

"Stop," the engineer warned, kneeling as close as he dared to the hole. He peered inside.

Instant silence prevailed.

"The walls are going," he said. "There's nothing we can do."

Tracy hung suspended, the blood rushing to her head as she swayed in her upside-down position. The world was collapsing all around her. *Judd,* she thought, and was filled with love and pity for him.

She knew then that she would never willingly leave him, no matter what he said. Maybe he wouldn't trust her again with his heart, but he needed her as much as she needed him. She realized that now. Together they were complete. Apart... life was nothing. It was the simple truth.

Rocks and dirt flew past her, pummeling her body as they fell into an endless darkness her light couldn't reach. Sometimes she couldn't tell if she were going upward or falling with the collapsing earth. Strangely, she wasn't afraid.

Because Judd was above her, taking care of her.

When their upward progress really did stop, she held on, waiting, knowing they were in safe hands... Judd's hands... his big, wonderful, tender hands.

When they didn't move for a minute, she grew a little worried. She didn't know how much longer she could hang on. Her shoulders were burning against the harness as she clung to consciousness.

The rocks stopped falling. The silence seemed to scream all around her. She breathed deeply. "Hold on," she tried to say. "Just hold on. Judd will get—"

The earth gave another rumble, a low growl of rage. The sides of the air shaft buckled against her and sent her swaying, banging from side to side. Then she was trapped as the ground started pressing against her, harder and harder.

What was going on? Why weren't they pulling her out?

She couldn't free her hand to jerk on the rope. But her feet could move. With all her might, she yanked her toes down and bent her knees at the same time.

Pull. Now.

She sent the thought to Judd, unable to speak as the earth shifted and lurched, filling her mouth, eyes and nose with debris as it fell into the eternity of darkness.

Got to hold on. Judd, help.

She felt a gigantic heaving. It was the end, she thought, and regretted all the things she hadn't told Judd...like how very much she loved him. *Oh, love, my love, my dearest love,* she repeated as the suffocating dust filled her lungs.

Thirteen

"**T**race!" Judd shouted. He grasped the rope, using every ounce of muscle he had to get Tracy free of the landslide. There was a second's resistance, then the rope began to move. He prayed it wouldn't break under the strain.

Behind him, Sterling winched in the slack, following his lead on the amount of tension to maintain. Judd pulled steadily, working hand over hand as the rope emerged from the dust cloud that rose from the collapsing air shaft. He stepped back when the edge where he was standing began to fall in.

Across from him, Jimmy's mother was screaming hysterically. Kane Hunter, who'd come out with the trauma team when Jimmy had been reported found, hurried over to her.

The roar increased. Judd couldn't tell if the sound was coming from the earth or from the frantic pounding of his heart. *Oh, God, not Trace,* he prayed. He couldn't bear to lose her a second time.

A foot appeared in the dust. Another. He reached for them, grabbing Tracy's ankles and yanking her out and to the side, away from the danger. The mining engineer helped him haul her to safety. A shout went up from those watching the drama.

Tears stung his eyes when he saw what had surprised the others gathered around the rim of the shaft. Tracy, unconscious, held on to Jimmy's ankles with a death grip. She'd brought the boy out with her.

"God, what a woman," Sterling said in admiration.

Judd dropped to his knees beside her.

Kane was already there. "Stay back," he ordered everyone. He freed her hands from the boy, then he and the paramedics got to work. First he did a Heimlich maneuver on her, while someone else did the same on Jimmy.

Dust puffed out from Tracy's mouth. She dragged in a breath of air, then was racked by coughs as her body tried to get rid of the debris she'd inhaled.

In a minute Jimmy, too, was coughing helplessly. Everyone cheered as if the two had won an Olympic event.

Oxygen masks were clamped over their faces. Their vital signs were checked, then both of them were loaded into the ambulance for the trip to the hospital. Jimmy had a broken arm to be set. Both of them would have to be watched for a few days, Kane explained, in case of complications.

Judd wanted to go to the hospital with Tracy, but he had other duties. "This area has to be secured and warnings posted about the danger of possible cave-ins." He looked at Dugin Kincaid, who owned the ranch now.

Mary Jo Kincaid touched Judd's arm. "Duggie said there used to be a sapphire mine somewhere on the old Baxter ranch. I understand they're used in medical research now and are quite valuable." She gave him a melting smile. "Wouldn't it be exciting if this was it...that something good came of a near tragedy?"

"It isn't." A member of the search team spoke up. Judd saw it was Rafe Rawlings. "Homer Gilmore has prospected this area. This was an old copper mine. It never produced anything worthwhile," the young cop explained.

Mary Jo looked disappointed. Judd frowned impatiently.

"I can finish up here," Sterling said. "Why don't you go on to the hospital? You might get your cast looked at while you're there," he advised with a puckish grin.

Judd gave him a grateful glance. "Thanks." He headed for his truck, but when a pain raced up his leg, he looked down. The cast had cracked from the pressure he'd exerted while pulling Tracy out, and had split nearly in two. He'd probably broken his leg again. It was a small price to pay, he thought, in exchange for two lives.

At the emergency department of the hospital, Judd found Tracy had already been taken to a room. She was in the shower. Kane took one look at him, shook his head and gestured toward the X-ray lab with his head.

"Let's get that leg taken care of, then you can see her. In fact, I'll put you both in the same room."

"I don't need to stay in the hospital," Judd growled.

"Tracy will want you close during the night. You may as well be comfortable."

After getting cleaned up and having a fresh cast put on his leg, Judd was taken to Tracy's room in a wheelchair in spite of his protests.

"Judd!" she exclaimed. "Are you all right? Where are you hurt?" She had to stop her anxious questions when a cough overtook her.

Light rushed into his heart, making him feel warm and new. He got out of the wheelchair and went to her, needing to hold her. Not giving a damn if the hospital gown hiked up and showed his behind to the nurses, he bent over and took her in his arms.

"I love you," he murmured, for her ears alone.

The nurses giggled and hurriedly left the room.

Tracy looked stunned. She touched his face. He noted her hand trembled. Her expression was a little wary, her smile wobbly.

He'd done that to her, he realized. Maybe she'd never been sure of his love. He hadn't mentioned it. He'd thought deeds were enough—marrying her, building the house, making love. He saw that he'd been wrong. She needed the words.

"I love you with everything in me. I always have. Someday I hope you'll believe that." He kissed her gently, briefly, aware of the oxygen tube clipped to her nose. There were so many things to say, so many things he'd like to do with her.

"Judd," she said in wonder. Her voice was hoarse from the coughing. It hurt him that she'd been hurt.

"You were right. There's something special between us. Love, that's what it is. God, Trace," he whispered. "I thought I would die. To lose you again after just finding you…"

"Shh," she said. "I know. Oh, love, I know."

After that, he lay on her bed and held her close, content to have her warm and safe beside him. He watched her become drowsy.

Just before she fell asleep, her eyes widened. "Oh, Judd, the most wonderful thing! I found the skull. It's in my knapsack on your desk. Can you start a check of the dental records right away?" She gazed at him earnestly before she started coughing.

Judd threw back his head and laughed. "I love you, you bone-crazy woman. I love you," he repeated, more softly this time.

Jimmy went home the second day, but Tracy developed pneumonia and spent five days in the hospital. Judd visited her each morning at six. He brought lunch each day at noon. He had dinner with her each night at five, then a snack at nine before he went home.

Her father came to visit. Lily Mae Wheeler invited him to her house for a home-cooked meal. Tracy giggled, then coughed for five minutes when her father, looking slightly dazed, and Lily Mae, smugly pleased, showed up for visiting hours the third evening of her hospital stay.

Tracy wondered if she should warn her parent that Lily Mae had designs on him, but decided against it. As Winona had noted, the widow wasn't the worst thing that could happen to a person.

Winona sneaked a jar of blackberry wine and another of chamomile tea up to her. Tracy's cough improved right away. Even Kane was impressed.

On Thursday, Judd took her home. He held her arm possessively as he guided her into the house, dragging his crutches in his left hand and limping on the new cast, which was covered with signatures of friends who'd visited him and Tracy that week. Jimmy's careful scrawl was included.

Once she was in bed, he served the supper Lily Mae had prepared and left in the oven. He'd already put out the word, through Sterling and Jessica for the townsfolk and Jackson and Maggie for the Cheyenne, that he didn't want company on their first night home.

"This is delicious," Tracy said, scooping up every bite as if they hadn't been swamped with wonderful home-made treats all week.

Every patient in the hospital had had fresh fry bread and honey for dessert that week, not to mention candy, cakes, cookies, fried chicken, sausage biscuits and everything else that Tracy had ever mentioned being fond of. She was the heroine of the hour with the news media and had received an award from the governor.

But now it was his moment, and he wanted no interruptions.

Judd removed the trays from the room and returned to sit on the bed beside her. He took her hand and cleared his throat.

"Do you know what next Tuesday is?" he asked, feeling almost reverent about the occasion.

"Yes," she answered, but said no more.

"Our wedding anniversary."

A flicker of emotion passed over her face and was gone before he could read it. She looked away. "Yes."

He cleared his throat again. He'd sort of *told* her they would be married the other time; this time he wanted to do it right.

"Trace. Tracy Roper Hensley," he said, starting over in formal tones. "Will you do me the honor of becoming my wife again?"

Her smile, tremulous and beautiful, bloomed on her face. "I'd like that very much," she said solemnly. "Oh, Judd, I'd like that very, very much."

He reached for her then, unable to stop himself. The kiss was meant to be gentle, a reaffirmation of his love, his commitment to her, this woman of his heart, but she was having none of that.

As in their first wild coming together, she tugged at him, demanding passion, wanting him with the same hunger he felt for her. He went dizzy with the pure joy of it.

"Ah, Trace," he whispered, savoring her taste, the sweet enchantment of her skin as he kissed her throat, sucked at her plump nipples, making them hard under his tongue.

He moved down to her waist and circled her belly button with his tongue, then delved into that sensitive dimple. He heard her gasp, and her hands roamed restlessly through his hair. He found the wonderful delight of her womanhood, that tiny nub that brought such pleasure to her and such joy to him.

He chuckled as she writhed under his ministrations, knowing he was driving her mad. He found great happiness in the task, loving the scent and taste, the texture and heat of her body as he showed her his love in every way he could.

When she cried out and went still, he waited, barely touching her with his tongue, until she moved again. He rose and moved between her thighs.

"No," she said weakly.

He paused. To his surprise, she pushed him down on the mattress of the queen-size bed that they'd shared in married bliss so long ago. Her gaze filled with love, she bent over him and gave him the same pleasure he'd given to her. He closed his eyes as love and happiness too strong to contain burst over him.

"Now, my love," she said when he could take no more. She moved over him and took him into her. It felt like coming home.

He placed his hands at her waist and guided her, smiling when she arched back and climaxed again. The passion flowed like a river between them. He caught the current and went with the flow.

Tracy woke to the *step-thump* of Judd approaching her side of the bed. He had a tray in his hands. The Sunday paper was under his arm.

"You're spoiling me," she scolded, looking at eggs fixed just the way she liked them and English muffins toasted to perfection.

"Not for long." He grinned. "Monday I'll expect you back on the job. You still haven't identified those bones."

She wrinkled her nose at him. "Slave driver. Haven't the men been working on it this week?"

"Yes. I thought you might feel up to helping out. No match was found in the records of the two dentists who have been in town for thirty years and still have an office, but we found a box of records in storage from another dentist. Old Doc Webster was the only dentist in town for years. He was eighty before he retired."

"Oh, good. And yes, I'd love to look through his records."

They chatted about the case while they ate their meal. "What about your job?" he asked later. "You have a dig—"

"I'll cancel it."

"No, you can't do that. You've worked too hard to get where you are to give it up. I'll just have to be patient—"

"If you'll be patient now, I'd explain it to you," she told him. "My father and I have been trying to arrange our schedules so we can write some books together. I'd like to do that. I'd also like to continue to be a consultant to the FBI. They usually have all the bones assembled when I'm called in on a case. At my prices, they usually can't afford to have me digging around in the dirt. As for the dig, there are plenty of people who can fill in for me."

Judd laughed, then became solemn. "I want you to be happy. If you want to go on digs, then you should."

She kissed him. "Thank you, my love."

After he cleaned up the dishes, he read the funny papers to her. He paused once when he looked up and saw the tears she couldn't hide.

"Would you like me to stop?" he asked, fighting his own memories of Sundays with her and Thadd.

She shook her head.

He finished, then refilled their cups from the insulated pitcher he'd brought in and placed on the lamp table. "By the way," he said casually, "Kane did our blood tests while we were in the hospital. The mayor volunteered to perform the ceremony.

"Oh?" she assumed an air of casual interest.

"He'll probably insist on making a production of it in the middle of town on the courthouse steps with all the TV and radio stations in attendance. I thought Tuesday. What do you think?"

"Tuesday," she repeated. "That's our anniversary."

"Yeah, that way we won't have to remember two dates," he explained with great practicality. Then he grinned.

Tracy held the door for Judd while he maneuvered through on his crutches. She helped him into his chair and laid the crutches close by so he could reach them easily. Then she hurried into the conference room, leaving the door open.

The box of dental records was on the table. The skull was there, too, grinning morosely at her as she took a chair. She studied the fillings in the teeth, then lifted out the first record. It belonged to Lexine Baxter. She studied Lexine's dental chart and wondered about the girl who had disappeared.

No one had given a damn about her, it seemed. Tracy found that sad. She glanced at the skull. She wondered if anyone had cared about him.

The next record was for a man who would have been about the right age. She noted the last name was Thomas. The records obviously weren't in alphabetical order. Looking at the careless way they'd been inserted into the storage box, she realized someone had probably spilled the folders and stuffed them back again as quickly as possible.

She sighed. It was going to be a long day.

At noon, Rafe Rawlings showed up carrying three bag lunches from the Hip Hop Café. He gave one to Judd and joined Tracy at the conference table.

"How's it going?" He eyed the stack of records she'd already gone through.

"No luck so far."

"You sound discouraged."

She smiled. "I'm not, but this is practically our last hope. I really wanted to solve this case."

"Yeah."

"Are you looking for clues to your parents?" she asked.

He shrugged. "It would be nice to know where I came from," he admitted.

"A young woman in trouble," she told him gently.

His lack of biological roots had made him an outsider in many ways, she realized. He was wary of people and involvement. Lily Mae had said he didn't have a regular girl.

"That's almost always the case with an abandoned baby. The father usually doesn't know about the child."

"Or doesn't care if he does know," Rafe added, picking up his sandwich and taking a bite with stoic calm.

Tracy felt he hid much behind that placid exterior.

Judd spoke from his desk. "Did you think there might be a connection between you and the bones?"

Rafe shrugged. "I was found in the woods—not the same ones, but close enough. There was a possibility. When Tracy told me the blood type, though, I knew it was no go. I'm negative. The bones were positive."

"That doesn't mean anything," Tracy told him.

"Wouldn't both parents have to be negative for the child to be? Doesn't the positive factor override the negative one?"

"Yes, if those two genes meet in the child. But two positive parents can have a negative-blood-type child if they both carry the recessive gene."

"But the chance is less likely."

She nodded and bit into the thick sandwich of ham and sprouts with a savory dressing that was low-fat and delicious.

After Rafe left, Judd called her to him. She went and sat in his lap. They napped for twenty minutes. The secretary returned from lunch and walked in, waking them.

"Oh-oh," she said. "Look, Boss, you're going to have to start locking the door if you're going to make out in the office."

Sterling walked in behind her. He flashed his badge. "Vice squad. I'm investigating a hot tip about kissing and..." There was a dramatic pause "...other stuff going on in public offices. Looks like I caught you red-handed with the goods on you."

Tracy snickered as Sterling eyed her sternly. She liked being the "goods" found on Judd.

"You have the right to remain silent," Sterling intoned, reading from his wallet card.

Judd threw a pencil eraser at his best detective. "Get out of here, or you'll find yourself on night patrol up in the mountain pass for the winter."

"Hey, you don't have to take it personally," Sterling protested. He headed for the exit.

"By the way, you want to be my best man on Tuesday?" Judd called before he got out the door.

Sterling stopped at Judd's casual question. "Yes...*hell* yes," he said. He let out a whoop. "Wait till I tell Jessica.

She and Maggie have a bet going about the wedding date. Jessica said before the month was over. Looks like she won.''

After he and the secretary left, Judd turned to Tracy. "The whole town will know by suppertime. Who's going to be your best woman?''

"Winona. Or do you think I should ask Lily Mae, in case she ends up as my stepmother?''

"Winona. Though I think we're going to see a lot of Lily Mae in the future. God, I never thought she'd be a possible mama-in-law.''

"Well, she hasn't wrestled him down the aisle yet.''

A short while later Tracy returned to her task. She worked the rest of the day and got a bit over halfway through the long box. When Judd stuck his head in the door, she was ready to go. She put the file she'd just picked up back in the box.

On the drive home, she wondered how it was possible to be so happy... and yet sad. Judd had asked her to marry him, but he was holding back, too. He was still guarding his heart.

The next day, dressed in a hurriedly bought silk outfit in her favorite golden yellow color from a new boutique near the Hip Hop Café, Tracy stood on the courthouse steps with Judd.

The mayor stood between them and smiled at the press, his wife at Judd's side. Lightbulbs flashed and camera whirred as the news media took advantage of the photo opportunity thus provided of the heroine and the sheriff... who happened to be her ex-husband as well as her soon-to-be new husband.

"It's so romantic," Tracy heard one reporter exclaim.

"It'll make the national news," another predicted with great satisfaction. He stepped closer with a mike when the mayor opened the book of marriage vows and took his place.

Winona leaned close to Tracy. "I told you you'd stay."

"Nobody likes people who say 'I told you so,'" she whispered back. She kissed the older woman's cheek. "But I love you just the same."

Winona wore a blue silk dress the color of the Montana sky. Her hair was neatly braided and wrapped around her head. She wore shoes and stockings and a discreet crystal necklace. On her shoulder was an orchid, pinned there by Judd who also planted a kiss on her cheek.

On the white Bible Tracy held, a red rose and a white one, their stems entwined, were the only adornment.

When the vows were over, the entire county went across the street to the park for a cookout. The meal was followed by cake and punch and a few fireworks, which were illegal, but the sheriff didn't arrest his chief deputy or the young cop who helped set them off.

Lightheaded from champagne, Tracy held on to Judd when they were dropped off at their house by a grinning rookie cop, who left in a hurry when his boss scowled at him.

Judd decided he should carry Tracy across the threshold. He made it, but stumbled one step inside the door. They went down in a tumble. One of the crutches barked him on the shin of his good leg. He cursed soundly.

"A fine way to talk," Tracy scolded. "How will it sound to our grandchildren when they learn their grandfather dropped his bride and cussed like a Montana miner on his wedding day?"

He quit rubbing his leg. "What grandchildren?"

She drew a slow breath. "The ones our child will probably have." She gave him a sweet smile that trembled only a little and waited anxiously for his response.

Judd stared into Tracy's eyes and realized this wasn't a joke. Emotion roiled within him. Another child. A picture of Thadd, still and lifeless, rushed into his mind. He sat up and rubbed a hand over his face, shutting out the pain of that nightmare.

A child. He hadn't counted on that. He'd thought... if it was just him and Trace, with no other complications... he'd thought he could live with that, deal with it if anything happened to her. But to start over... to go through it all again...

"Judd?"

She touched him lightly on the arm and withdrew. He had to look at her then. Her skin, always pale as fresh milk, seemed whiter and drawn against the fine bones of her face. Her gaze was anxious... and pleading.

God, did she know what she was asking him?

"Are you sure you're pregnant?" he asked. He didn't recognize his own voice, it was so strained.

She nodded and visibly swallowed. Her hands plucked nervously at her wedding dress. She removed her hat with the net that covered half her face, laid it on a chair, then slipped out of her satin shoes and pushed them aside.

Without looking at him, she sat quietly, staring out the open door. Her face was still, as still as death... *no*, don't think that. Oh, God, to go through it again... to love a child.

"How... when? You've known... for how long?" He was stalling for time, for some insight to tell him how to deal with this.

"When I was in the hospital," she said. "I felt queasy, so I asked Kane to do the test."

"The pregnancy test," Judd mumbled, looking stunned.

"Yes."

"I thought . . . after Thadd . . ." He gestured helplessly.

"Yes. The doctors said it would be difficult, perhaps impossible, for me to conceive. And I didn't during all those years. Oh, Judd," she cried softly, "it's like a miracle. We'll be a family again, like we were . . ."

Tracy stopped at the grimace of pain that crossed his face. She watched anxiously as he gripped one crutch like a lifeline. She hadn't realized it would be so hard on him to accept the idea of another family. It was too soon. She hadn't prepared him for fatherhood again.

"Please, say something." Fear ate at her, and she could hardly speak. "Please say you want it—our child. . . . I need you to say it. . . ." Her world teetered on the brink of destruction.

He reached for her then. Pulling her close, he buried his face in her hair. She felt a shudder run through his hard, lean frame and she wrapped her arms around him, wanting to comfort him.

"It'll be all right," she whispered. "It will, Judd."

"I know," he said at last. "I know."

He took her face between his hands and gazed into her eyes. "I do want the child. It was . . . for a minute, I thought of the risk. . . ."

"The risk of childbirth?" She'd had an easy birth. Judd knew that. He'd been with her throughout the labor.

"The risk of loving. I remembered how it felt to lose our son, and then to lose you. I thought of going through that again."

"You'll never lose me." She realized she couldn't give total guarantees for the future. "Life can be dangerous. I can't promise it won't be, but I'll never voluntarily leave you."

He laid a finger over her lips. "That day at the mine, when you went down for Jimmy, I thought if you died, then it would be over for me. The pain of it, Trace, God, the pain."

She made a little sound, trying to soothe and reassure him. She knew the anguish he spoke of.

He sighed. "That's a coward's way of thinking. There's always a risk in living. In loving, too."

His gaze held hers. She listened with all her heart while he sorted through his feelings, knowing this moment was vital to their future happiness. She wanted complete commitment from him now, for her and her love and for their child.

"Kids are curious beings," he went on. "They go off on their own to explore the world. That's natural."

"Yes." She realized Judd was accepting the past as she had that day in the cemetery. Like her, he was facing the sorrow, the pain, and letting it go. She held very still and waited.

"Things happen—car wrecks, cave-ins, fire, flood. The world is full of disaster. It's on the nightly news. But there are a thousand other moments, each one precious, each one blessed with love and joy. That's what I forgot with Thadd. The joy of knowing him. I remembered only the pain." He touched his forehead to hers. "Forgive me, my love."

"For what—being human?"

"I told you in the hospital I loved you. I've told you I didn't want to live when I thought you might die. But it wasn't the whole truth. You see, I thought I could love you a little bit. That it would be safe if things didn't get too involved. As long as it was just the two of us, without other complications."

"And then you learn about a new baby," she murmured, seeing what he was getting at. She'd sensed he was holding back, but she'd thought it was because he didn't completely trust her love yet. She'd thought, with time, it would come.

He gave a wry, husky laugh. "Life doesn't work in half measures, it seems."

"I'm sorry," she said, the words strained. "I didn't mean to make it so hard for you—"

"No," he said, cutting off her apology. "Don't be sorry. I want this child. I want you and our love and everything that love can possibly offer. I want it all, Trace. Everything."

Looking into his eyes, she saw he meant it. The barriers were completely gone. Love gleamed in those dark depths, bright as the rising sun...bright as all the tomorrows to come.

She lifted her face and felt his kiss on her mouth. A pledge, she realized, to the future, to their children.

Now...now she felt she was truly his wife, each of them part of the other and of the whole fabric of life.

"Where were we?" he asked. "Oh, yes, I was about to ravish you, Mrs. Hensley."

They made love there on the floor at eight o'clock on a late summer's evening with the door wide open. Fortunately, all the neighbors were still at the party.

Fourteen

Tracy woke at dawn. Judd was tickling her nose with the corner of the blanket. She laughed, pushed his hand away and scratched the offended part.

"What do you want to do today?" he asked.

"Well," she drawled, "what did you have in mind?"

"We've never had a honeymoon," he reminded her. He combed her tangled curls with his fingers. "The first time we couldn't afford it. But now we can. I'd like to take you somewhere special, to a place you've always wanted to go, but never had the chance."

"There's only one place," she said softly. "It's here, in your arms. From the moment I met you, this is where I've longed to be. Always." She caressed his strong jaw and ran her thumb over his lips. "For me, this is paradise."

They stayed in bed another hour, and Judd said all the things she wanted to hear, the special things that lovers say. She loved it that he opened himself to her and expressed his feelings, and she told him so.

"If only we'd talked before," he said at one point.

She laid a hand over his mouth. "No regrets," she ordered. "We look forward from this moment on."

"No regrets," he agreed. His kiss was his promise.

"Well, look who's here—the folks who ran out on their own wedding party." Sterling laid a report on the secretary's desk and followed the couple into the other room.

"It was either that or arrest half the town, including the chief deputy, for disturbing the peace." Judd hung his hat on a peg and hobbled over to his chair.

Tracy grinned at the two and left them. Going into the small conference room, she plunked her purse on a chair, took her seat and picked up where she'd left off two days ago. Today she would finish the box of records.

A tingle of excitement shot through her as she lifted the next file, opened it, glanced at the macabre grin on the skeleton and looked at the dental record.

A filling in a molar matched, she saw. And another. And another. The root canal in a bicuspid was the same. The lower back molars had been extracted, according to the dental chart. The lower back molars were missing from the skull.

"Judd!" she yelled. "Sterling!"

The two men stopped their monthly planning session and peered through the open door at her.

"I've found him!" she said. "I've found our cow-boy!"

Both men leapt to their feet and stampeded into the room. One on each side, they peered over her shoulders.

"Look." She pointed to each detail on the chart and on the teeth in the skull. Every one was the same.

"What's the name?" Judd demanded. "Who is it?"

She turned the card over and peered at the information side. "Charles Avery," she read. "Oh..."

"What just occurred to you?" Judd asked, his eyes narrowed on her as if she were the suspect in the case.

"He was the one...Lily Mae told me about him and the Baxter girl who used to live here. Everyone thought they'd run off together. That was about twenty-eight years ago. Oh, Judd, Melissa Avery from the Hip Hop Café—the bones...they belong to her father."

"Hmm," Sterling mused aloud, "did she kill him?"

"Melissa? She couldn't have. She was just a baby at the time," Tracy explained.

Sterling gave her a pained look. "I meant the woman he was supposed to have run off with."

"Lexine Baxter?"

"She would have had to be pretty strong to have killed him with a rock," Judd said.

"She wasn't an Amazon type, not that I remember," Tracy put in. "I don't think Avery was dead when he was pushed under the ledge. Remember, I found blood in the soil there? He could have been in a daze, then gone into a coma."

"And bled to death," Sterling concluded.

"Winona saw our cowboy...Charles Avery," Tracy amended. "She saw him fighting with another man. Maybe that was who did him in and left him to die."

"But who was that?" Judd frowned, then gave Sterling a wicked grin. "I know just the man to put to work on a twenty-eight-year-old murder mystery."

Sterling said a rude word.

The telephone rang. Tracy hit the speaker button. "Tracy Roper...Hensley," she said in her official voice, grinning at Judd's scowl.

"Tracy, I have some news for you."

"Winona," Tracy said warmly. She had news of her own. "We know who the cowboy was. I found his dental records. You'll never guess in a million years—"

Winona wasn't the least interested in the past. "It's a girl," she said smugly. "But the next one will be a boy."

*   *   *   *   *

Montana Mavericks

continues with
THE RANCHER TAKES A WIFE

by Jackie Merritt
Available in December

Here's an exciting preview....

One

Melissa froze at the sudden knock on her door. Who could be visiting at this time of the night? She saw a man's silhouette. "Wyatt," she whispered with a sinking sensation, though she was identifying him from form alone. But she *knew* it was him. For a moment she couldn't think.

She drew a shaky breath. "Who is it? Who's there?"

"Wyatt. Please open the door."

A crazy thrill shot through her body, alarming her. He was married and he had hurt her and why in God's name would she feel anything but revulsion for him?

Stay calm, she told herself.

She crossed to the door, unlocked it and opened it a few inches. "What do you want, Wyatt?" The light by the door revealed his features, his handsome face and his eyes, which she had once used to gauge his moods. A dark, chocolate brown, Wyatt's eyes had always silently spoken his thoughts. Right now they contained an impassioned plea.

"Just some conversation. A few minutes of your time. Please let me come in."

She looked away. "We have nothing to talk about."

"Melissa, please don't send me away." She was wearing a robe and her hair was loose and he could see the hairbrush in her hand. Standing this close to her was a sweet kind of torture. He had loved her so much, her laughter, her kisses and as easily as striking a match it could all be ignited again. For him, anyway.

"I only want to talk," he said quietly, which was the truth—for now.

What he wanted to do, Melissa thought unhappily, was to apologize in person for marrying another woman. Did she want to hear that? Could she bear hearing that? What difference would another apology make, anyhow? It was long in the past and irrevocable.

But she couldn't refuse him. He was still Wyatt, the boy and then the man she had loved with all her heart and soul.

She stepped back and led him to the living room. There was an uncomfortable silence as they searched for something to say.

"What do you want to talk to me about?" she asked, rather brusquely.

Wyatt raised one booted foot to rest on his other knee. "Did you hear about my divorce?"

Melissa's eyes widened. "When did that happen?"

Wyatt cleared his throat. "Actually, it's in progress. It won't be final for a few more weeks."

Melissa's mouth was suddenly dry as dust. Surely he wasn't thinking that his divorce would mean something to her, like maybe she would be glad to hear about it. She wasn't. There was at least one child involved, and having grown up as an "abandoned" child—other people's opinion, not hers—she hated the idea of a family breaking up. She had always imagined Wyatt would be a good father. They had talked about children—*their* children. It hurt so much to remember all that now.

Damn him. Did he actually have the gall to think there could be anything between *them* again?

"Melissa, I never stopped ... missing you," he said softly.

She got to her feet. "That's unfortunate for you, Wyatt. I stopped missing you about six years ago. I don't want to hear it." To her dismay, despite her anger, something inside of her was responding to his good looks—his long, lean body and his eyes. *Damn* his eyes for being so expressive.

"Melissa, you're special—"

"Yeah, right," she said coldly. "You proved *how* special, Wyatt, so please don't lay any phony lines on me."

She became aware of his gaze on her robe and defiantly tugged the sash tighter. "Go home, Wyatt. There's nothing for you here."

"Nothing at all, Melissa? You never married," he said softly. She was beautiful and bright and he had never stopped loving her. True, she wasn't the same sweet, malleable girl he remembered. Her air of independence and self-reliance was almost tangible. But just being in the same room with her made his blood run faster.

"That's right. I never married. But don't make the mistake of thinking it had anything to do with you." She led the way back to the hall and reached for the door knob.

But she hadn't realized how closely he followed and nearly jumped out of her skin when she felt his hand in her hair. For the merest fraction of time she permitted the thrills to compound in her body. His fingers moving in her hair felt like heaven on earth. Then she whirled around. "How dare you touch me like that?"

His eyes were dark and hooded. "Will you go out with me?" he asked.

"No, absolutely not."

"Afraid of me, Melissa? Are you afraid of what I'm making you feel?"

She tried to scoff. "You have too much ego, Wyatt. The only thing you're making me feel is uncomfortable."

"That's a lie. Don't you think a man knows when a woman is feeling all fluttery and excited because of him?"

Melissa's eyes suddenly blazed. "That's enough! How dare you come to my home, act like I should be glad to see you and then have the bloody gall to suggest . . . to suggest . . ." She couldn't say it. But he was talking about sex, damn him! As though she didn't have the strength of will to resist him.

She angrily poked him in the chest with her forefinger. "What you're interpreting as fluttering and excitement is plain shock that you'd have the brass to come here in the first place. I don't want—"

Her words stopped abruptly because his mouth was suddenly on hers. Sputtering, she pushed against him. But his hands were cradling her head and holding it right where he wanted it. His lips moved on hers, gently, then roughly, then gently again. She thought she might faint from shock and fury, when she'd never fainted in her life.

Her lips felt swollen and softly sensual when he finally stopped kissing them and raised his head to look into her eyes. "I didn't intend doing that when I came here tonight," he whispered. "But I'm not sorry about it. Melissa, you can deny it till hell freezes over, but there'll always be something between us. What I did to you can never be undone. God, if only it could. I never expected to see you again, but I'm not going to lose you a second time."